THE LEGEND OF COAL OIL JOHNNY

THE LEGEND OF COAL OIL JOHNNY

Richard W. Aites

iUniverse, Inc.
New York Lincoln Shanghai

THE LEGEND OF COAL OIL JOHNNY

iUniverse books may be ordered through booksellers or by contacting:

iUniverse
2021 Pine Lake Road, Suite 100
Lincoln, NE 68512
www.iuniverse.com
1-800-Authors (1-800-288-4677)

This is a work of fiction. All of the characters, names, incidents, organizations, and dialogue in this novel are either the products of the author's imagination or are used fictitiously.

ISBN: 978-0-595-45232-3 (pbk)
ISBN: 978-0-595-89540-3 (ebk)

Printed in the United States of America

THE EARLY HISTORY OF OIL

Petroleum was first used nearly forty centuries ago when the Ancient Egyptians utilized it in the preparation of mummies. The Hindu people used oil to treat disease and cremate corpses. The Ancient Chinese drilled, produced, and marketed natural gas which they used in their homes for lighting and heat; it was distributed through bamboo pipelines. Early Europeans also used petroleum for light.

Other kinds of oil have been used by many different cultures over the generations. As early as 800 A.D. the Basques hunted whales and used whale oil for light and heat. Over time, many products including paint, varnish, soap, candles, medicine, and lubricating fluids were crafted from whale oil. Eventually the demand exceeded the supply, and by the seventeenth century, shortages of whales and their valuable bodily fluid led to skirmishes between the Dutch and the English. Because of the scarcity of whales, whalers had to venture far beyond the reach of Europe in search of their prey. Eventually people realized that future supplies needed to be discovered elsewhere. 'Rock Oil' was the answer.

In this country, the Seneca Indians informed the early settlers about oil seeps. These Native Americans were actually the first oil producers on this continent. Centuries before Columbus landed upon the New World's shores, the Indians were collecting oil by trapping it in timber-lined pits near bubbling seeps along the banks of Oil Creek in northwestern Pennsylvania. The Seneca also skimmed the oil from the water's surface with blankets. They used the substance for both ceremonial and medicinal purposes.

Samuel M. Kier operated a salt well near Tarentum, Pennsylvania. He was a clever entrepreneur and inventor. In the 1840's, other salt-well operators became discouraged when their wells along the Allegheny River began to produce greasy crude oil. Kier, however, saw this as an opportunity. He created uses for the mucky substance that was contaminating the salt wells. He collected the oil and began selling it for medicinal purposes. The business became so successful that he began purchasing petroleum from other salt well operators.

Kier eventually experimented by refining crude oil into kerosene. The refining process decreased the amount of smoke emitted from burning crude. Improvements in the distillation (refining) process led to increased demands for the oil he collected. The finished product burned brightly, provided the necessary heat for warmth and cooking, and was cheaper than whale oil and lard. The Native American practice of skimming the oil springs was a tedious endeavor and produced very meager amounts of the precious substance. 'Col.' Drake considered boring a hole into the earth to obtain the crude oil. With the assistance of an experienced blacksmith and salt well driller, and the proper Tools to perform such a task, Drake drilled the first successful oil well near Titusville, Pennsylvania in August of 1859. It was here, in this serene little valley, where the mighty oil industry was born.

BOYHOOD

CHAPTER 1

A Rattler's Welcome

I was about ten when my family settled into the Oil Creek valley. Though my weathered face and trembling hands never fail to remind me of my eighty-plus years, my mind and memory are nearly as sharp now as back then.

My Father, an Irishman and farmer, had inherited several acres of land along the now historic creek. The land was rough, infertile, and riddled with boulders. Gray stones the size of wagons were scattered throughout the steep hillsides surrounding our meager inheritance. I later learned that the megaliths were the remnants of an ice age that were deposited thousands of years earlier by mighty glaciers creeping southward. These same mountains of ice carved out the Allegheny Valley.

My father was a hardy man, and it wasn't long before he turned the stony acres into a productive little plot. Maize and beans were our main crops, but my mother had planted a garden behind the cabin which was much more diverse in nature. She grew peppers of several sorts, giant pumpkins, tasty butternut squash, and onions that were sweeter than wild ones.

Times were pretty good, especially for a young boy who enjoyed the simple pleasures of country living. The Allegheny foothills that surrounded our sparse settlement teemed with rabbits, squirrels, wildcats (bobcats), and game birds. The creek itself was full of bass, yellow-bellied catfish, and speckled trout. Vanes of the sweetest berries grew along the stream's rocky embankment, and chestnut trees abounded in the dense forest behind our farm. I loved to hunt and fish and my family had been the beneficiary of paradise.

It wasn't long before my curiosity got the better of me and I began to explore the land on the opposite side of the creek. One early spring day while fishing at the mouth of Cherry Run, I stepped out of the icy water and climbed up onto the cluttered embankment, where I removed my moccasins to allow my feet to dry in the warm, noonday sun. As I plopped down on a large piece of driftwood I was startled by the amplified sound of a baby's rattle. I cautiously turned my head and trembled in fear when I observed not one, but two large rattlesnakes just a few feet beyond the log on which I sat. The coiled vipers were angry because I was a trespasser in their rocky domain.

Still trembling, I silently begged Providence to spare me, while I kept my eye on the agitated reptiles. Shortly I felt some small relief as the smaller of the two rattlers retreated into a nearby crevice created by a pile of brush and stones. The larger serpent was more reluctant to give up his ground, and even began to inch closer to me backside. I was horrified as I peered into his fiery, red eyes. As the snake raised his scaly head to target my left buttock, I again begged God to save me.

Just as the snake's head was poised to thrust, a human hand darted out of nowhere and grasped the venomous critter just behind the head. The fearless young fellow allowed the serpent to coil its three-foot long body around his arm before kissing the reptile on top of the head.

The tall, lanky lad then used his free hand to unwrap the snake, and tossed it several feet into the warmer water of Oil Creek. A small, scruffy dog ran up from behind the boy and immediately jumped into the creek in an attempt to retrieve the poisonous critter. "Weasel! Let that bastard be! You already done kilt' three of 'em taday," the angry boy hollered. The little canine turned and doggy paddled back ashore; the sopping mutt jumped up onto the log beside me and shook its shaggy coat, showering me with dirty creek water.

I thanked the lad for saving my life. "He wouldn't have eaten much. Jus' tryin' to impress his lady friend, is all. Nasty cusses are breedin' right now, ya know." He then introduced himself as John Washington Steele, but he informed me that most just called him Johnny. "I'm Andrew Buchanan. Live down the creek a ways. Just moved here from Potter County." We shook hands and proceeded about a half-mile up the creek to the McClintock farm. The farm was enormous, several times larger than our own. It was the product of nearly a decade of hard work and cultivation by Culbertson McClintock and his wife Sarah, who were both very fine people.

From that day on, life in the solitary valley became one big adventure, an adventure that would create a legend.

CHAPTER 2

Darned Bear!

Later that same spring, Sarah McClintock sent Johnny and me out to retrieve a prize hog that had wandered from the farm. It was unusually hot, so she figured that the old sow had moseyed down to the creek to wallow in the cool water. With the sun directly overhead, we crossed over the big flat that come autumn would be full of corn and buckwheat. Upon completion of the quarter-mile journey, we stood atop a ridge that overlooked a good stretch of the creek. It was June, and the foliage was so thick that what little of the creek bank we could see, revealed no hog. I momentarily became fixated on a great blue heron that was strutting along the shallows searching for a lunch of small fish and crustaceans. The elegant bird was nearly as tall as I.

Johnny decided that we needed a closer look, so we started down the steep, earthen slope. Almost instantly the dry soil beneath our feet gave way, causing a minor landslide. I crashed down onto my rear end, but the more agile Steele came to an abrupt halt near the foot of the slope. While I recovered my feet and patted the dirt and dust from my britches, Johnny was concentrating on something ahead. He peered back at me and placed his index finger across his lips. "Hear that?" he whispered in reference to a sudden movement within the blackberry patch below. The enormous patch of succulent berries covered nearly two acres and was shaded by several ancient oak and maple trees. The darkness created by the foliage of the mighty trees and the raspy clatter of crickets and katydids made for an eerie scene.

Confident that the disturbance from within was McClintock's hog, Johnny crept over to the edge of the patch. "You coming, Drew?" Fearing the unknown, I declined. I opted to hold my position just in case the old slab of bacon doubled back. Johnny smirked at my frivolous excuse and proceeded into the darkness ahead. He was gone a mere two minutes when I heard a great ruckus in the thorny entanglement. I was startled by the thunder of wings when several grouse exploded from the patch. As the hefty birds dispersed into the foliage above, a dead calm settled over the scene.

Moments later the bushes near the center of the patch began to sway as if dancing to a silent chorus. This was puzzling because it was a calm day without even a gentle breeze. As I peered deeper into the thicket to locate Johnny, he began shouting at the top of his lungs. I couldn't make out what he was saying, but there was panic in his voice.

Instantly Johnny burst from the patch like a half-starved heel hound after the last morsel of venison. The expression on his face was sheer terror as he dashed past me and clambered up the collapsing slope. As debris from his struggle rained down onto me, I reckoned that he had upset a hive of yellow jackets. Though terrified of wasps and bees, I remained still to avoid alerting the angry insects of my presence. Gazing back into the dense patch, I saw something that made the hair on the back of my neck stand straight up. A huge, dark mass was pummeling its way through the razor sharp, thorny vanes.

My blood froze when, not ten feet away, an old bear burst from the thick cover. His teeth were a-clickin' like hail on a new barn roof and long strands of saliva dangled from his mouth as he angrily pursued Johnny. In a moment the beast was on the boy's heels. I watched in disbelief as all eighty-five pounds of John Washington Steele desperately scurried up the dusty ridge with four-hundred pounds of irate black bear close behind.

I had been told by my father that a bear could run faster up a hill than down one, and now I was seeing the proof, at Steele's expense. "Darned bear!" Johnny hollered as he made his way up onto the flat before sprinting forward. The bear cleared the incline and was nearly on top of Johnny when the boy stopped dead in his tracks and turned to face down the charging beast. As the black bundle of fury closed to within scant feet, it skidded to a stop, its huge paws spraying decaying leaves and debris into the lad's face. Only the length of a tall man separated the two, and I figured Johnny was a goner. I was distraught at the prospect of dragging Johnny's half-eaten remains back to the farm, where I'd inform the loving Mrs. McClintock that her only son had been lunch for a bear.

Yet Johnny and that bear just stood there eye ballin' one another. Thinking that the bear was gonna pounce at any minute, I was shocked at what came next. Johnny danced around and hollered at the top of his lungs. I couldn't make out a word of it, but it was loud and annoying. The god-awful melody was so offensive that I forgot about being scared. Johnny just kept on a-hootin' and a-hollerin' while the bear stood his ground. The spectacle reminded me of a young warrior that had indulged in too much whiskey before partaking in one of the tribe's traditional war dances.

The ruckus was so discomforting that I had to cover my ears with cupped hands. I watched as the old bear stood upon its hind legs and raised its massive front paws above its huge head. The animal appeared more confused than I. It seemed to be pleading for young Steele to stop the awful exhibition. The bear suddenly dropped back down on all fours, turned, and high-tailed it for the creek. I watched as the retreating animal disappeared into a wall of honey-suckle and thistle at the far end of the ridge.

Relieved, the exhausted boy fell flat on his back before staring into the clear blue sky above. Still in total disbelief as to what had just transpired, I slowly gathered myself and eventually made my way up onto the flat. I plopped down next to Johnny. Moments later we heard a loud splash down at the creek. "Dang, Johnny. You messed that old bear up so bad, why he ran down to the 'crick' and drowned himself!"

Later that afternoon we found the old sow in a tiny marsh beyond the farm. A couple of deep lacerations to the hog's front shoulder indicated that the bruin was after some ham steaks. Unfortunately for the bear, he'd come across the orneriest creature this side of the Mississippi. The hog eventually recovered.

The following fall I told some of the local boys about our encounter with the bear. By the time the story reached our teacher, Mrs. Crosby, Johnny had whipped a thousand-pound Grizzly bear with his bare hands. Within our little one-room schoolhouse, John W. Steele was as much a part of history as the likes of Daniel Boone.

CHAPTER 3

The Shootist

The following summer I learned that young Steele was quite a marksman. One hot Sunday afternoon in Oakland Township, our church and its boisterous Pastor, Edgar Slentz, was sponsoring their annual meat shoot. The prize was a thirty-pound ham. Several of the menfolk showed up toting new-fangled percussion guns and rifled muskets. One fellow boasted that he could knock the fly off a horse's ass at fifty paces. Another fellow arrived with an elaborate longrifle adorned with fancy German silver inlays and a tiger maple stock. He had recently purchased the beautiful piece from a master craftsman in Lancaster County.

Johnny was the laughingstock of the congregation when he arrived toting an old English fowler that he had inherited from Mr. McClintock. The ungainly piece was longer than the boy was tall, even after his stepfather hacked a foot off the barrel. The ancient relic was equipped with a great big flintlock. Tucked in his belt was a dragoon pistol that shot lead balls as big as chestnuts. Steele had also inherited the horse pistol from Mr. McClintock.

Henry Rouse stepped up to the firing line. Some thirty paces below was a crabapple resting on the decaying stump of an oak. Rouse was originally from Enterprise, Pennsylvania but had settled into the area nearly a decade earlier. He owned one of the largest farms in the Oil Creek valley, and though he was not a wealthy man, a large herd of cattle and pigs allowed him and his family luxuries foreign to the rest of our little farming community. One of those luxuries was the fancy, new rifle he raised to his shoulder. The polished brass ornaments of the Hawken gleamed in the sunlight as the old man took aim on the target below. A loud boom echoed throughout the valley and a large chunk of the stump was turned into mulch, but the tiny apple did not budge. "Yah barely missed it, Mister Rouse!" one spectator remarked as Rouse lowered his rifle. The old farmer mumbled a few words in disgust as he left the firing line.

Johnny was the youngest participant, so he was last to shoot. Seven men had taken their best shot, but none had hit the fruit. When Steele stepped up to the firing line, most of the congregation chuckled at the skinny lad and his monstrous firearm. "That thang weighs more than he does!" One gent commented. "Right out of General Washington's war!" Another fellow hollered.

Johnny was not shaken by their comments. He raised the big musket and then looked over at the Mc Clintocks, who were standing at the sideline. Mr. McClintock gave the boy a nod and a surge of confidence. He focused onto the apple and steadied his aim. "Come on, boy! Shoot that ugly thang!" Elder Slentz shouted. Johnny paid no mind as he took a deep breath and gently squeezed the trigger. There was a 'swoosh' followed by a loud 'boom' as a cloud of sulphuric white smoke engulfed the boy's falling frame. The recoil from the mighty piece knocked Johnny onto his rear end. Some of the spectators chuckled as he picked himself up from the ground and wiped the dirt from the back of his britches. When the smoke cleared, the laughter subsided. The apple was gone. The big round ball from Johnny's musket had struck home, vaporizing the piece of bitter fruit. Sure disbelief, and the aroma of applesauce lingered about the air as the boy claimed his prize.

CHAPTER 4

Turkey for Supper

A couple of weeks following the annual meat shoot, Mr. Stephen Irwin delivered a wagonload of lumber to the farm. While helping him and my father unload the planks for our new barn, I overheard the old mill operator talking about a large flock of turkeys that were often seen roosting in the trees beyond his mill. "They be there jus' about every mornin'," The gritty Irishman proclaimed as he wiped the sweat from his bristly brow. "I aint much for huntin'. Like fishin' though," he announced. "Whad about you boy? You're big anuff to hunt. Ain't ya?" "Went huntin' with Johnny once," I replied. "The McClintock boy?" he asked. "Yes, sir!"

"I heard about him. He put them men folk to shame at that ham shoot," Irwin replied before spitting a glob of tobacco juice to the ground at his feet. "Now them turkey be in the tall oaks on the big hill, above my mill. You got to git up there early, though, to catch'em comin' down to feed." The old codger spat again. "Come spring, I'm gunna start makin' logs out of them trees." I focused on my father. "Can me and Johnny go huntin', Pa?" I anxiously asked. My father hesitated and wiped his sweaty neck. "As long as John Steele goes along," He replied. "Later this afternoon I'll go down into the cellar and fetch the shotgun," he added as he patted me on top of the head.

Later that evening, my father taught me how to shoot the old smoothbore. I fired the piece twice before my shoulder began to throb with pain. Though I was a stout boy for my age, the recoil from two more hefty loads of buckshot did my tender shoulder in. As for accuracy, I did manage to ventilate two rotting pumpkins.

After the marksmanship training, I dashed to the McClintock farm, where I informed Johnny about the old sawyer's revelation. "Wow! A whole flock, you say? Kilt a few grouse, but I ain't never got a turkey," Steele cheered.

The sun was just beginning to peek above the horizon when Johnny arrived at the farm on an old mare. A sack of grain was draped over the horse's shoulders and a musket strapped alongside. Favoring my sore shoulder, I was able to climb up onto the horse with a little help from Johnny. The painful grimace on my face gave it away. I told him I had injured it while unloading lumber.

We journeyed through the lonely woods surrounding Cherry Tree Run before reaching the mill some thirty minutes later. Mr. Irwin and his apprentice had just arrived, and the old Irishman pointed out the area where the tasty birds were mustering. The land surrounding the hillside had been cleared of timber. The hill itself was actually a small mountain. It was nearly as steep as Rynd Hill and I grew exhausted just looking at it. "Jus' over that crest is a grove of walnut and oak. Them birds be up there feedin' on acorns and such," the mill operator proclaimed.

Johnny tied the horse to a fledgling hickory tree near the mill shack. We then proceeded through a canyon of fallen limbs and rotting stumps before beginning our ascent of the steep incline. Halfway up we halted briefly so I could catch my breath. The eight-pound shotgun in my arms was beginning to feel more like eighty. We continued upward, and several minutes later we were nearing the top. I briefly stopped to turn and look back into the valley below. The mill was tiny, and appeared to be several miles away.

Another hundred yards and we reached the peak. We kneeled alongside a crooked sycamore and examined the forest ahead. Fifty yards beyond stood several acres of big trees. This was the grove the old man had told us about. "From here on, we need to be real quiet. The turkey is the wariest darned critter in the woods. If we spook'em, we'll never get a shot," Johnny whispered. We sat for a spell before I observed a movement on the forest floor. A fat squirrel was gorging itself on acorns in preparation for the long winter ahead. In a few short weeks the leaves would be turning to the fall colors of crimson and gold. The air would turn brisk, and the fresh scent of autumn would permiate through the valley. The animals would be active, fattening up for the trying season ahead. I adored the fall and its pleasant days and cool evenings. The fishing was always best this time of year.

It wasn't long before a half-dozen squirrels joined in on the smorgasbord. Growing impatient with the sound of rustling leaves and chattering tree rats, I suggested we shoot some of the bushytailed rodents. "Shush. We ain't shootin' no squirrels taday. I want a turkey for supper," Steele whispered. "We're too close to the ground. A turkey got eyes like a hawk, and they'll see us for sure if we stay put," he added. "What are we gonna do?" I asked. Johnny gazed into the thick foliage above. "We need to get up in the trees."

Against my better judgement, I was hoisted up onto the low-hanging limb of a sprawling maple. Though I was only eight feet off the ground, I had an excellent view of the surrounding forest. I leaned up against the thick trunk while resting the smoothbore across my lap. Meanwhile, Johnny quietly circled his way to the opposite side of the grove. I was amazed at how silent his footsteps were, considering the ground was cluttered with dried leaves, fallen limbs, and nuts. He was like an Indian stalking wild game. Johnny eventually found another tree with a relatively low-hanging limb and perched upon it. About 75 yards of scrub brush and tall hardwoods separated us.

It was about nine o'clock in the morning, and I was growing quite bored of watching squirrels cut nuts and birds flutter about the forest floor while snatching flying insects. "I should be fishin' right now," I mumbled to myself as I rested my head against the gnarled bark of the tree. It wasn't long before my eyes were shut and I was dreaming of fresh trout for dinner.

I hadn't been sleeping long when I was startled by the blast from Johnny's musket. I sat up and grabbed hold of the shotgun resting on my lap as I was instantly enveloped in an explosion of dark wings and feathers. The big bodies of several cackling turkeys busted through the underbrush below as I shoulder the smoothbore. As more and more birds took to flight, my aim was burdened by the distraction. Before I could fire, a squawking young hen struck me squarely in the chest. The impact knocked me completely off the limb and I plummeted to the ground below. I landed flat on my back, with every ounce of wind knocked out of my lungs.

Powerless, I watched as the big, clumsy birds continued flying overhead, in an attempt to escape their pursuer. A few minutes passed before I recovered and was breathing normally again. I sat up and was relieved that my back was not broken. Johnny approached me moments later with a smile upon his face. In one hand he carried his massive musketoon and in the other he was toting a huge gobbler.

When I started to regain my feet, Johnny hollered for me to stay put. Still dazed from my fall, I couldn't understand what he meant. "Stay down," he ordered as his eyes widened and he focused on something behind me. He tossed the dead gobbler onto the forest floor and shouldered his musket. He slowly cocked the hammer and told me to keep my head down. I trembled with fear as I imagined a bear or wolf ready to pounce. I ducked my head between my portly knees and prayed as Steele fired. I was consumed in a cloud of white smoke that slowly dissipated into the air above me. As the sulphuric smelling haze cleared, Johnny walked right past me to a spot some twenty yards beyond. He lifted another turkey from the ground. "Now we both got one!" he gleefully shouted as I staggered to my feet.

We later determined that while I was asleep, a flock of about thirty turkeys had moseyed into the grove while feeding on acorns and berries. Johnny waited patiently for the largest bird in the flock to present a good, clear shot. Upon dispatching the twenty-five pound bird, the rest of the flock took to the wing to escape. The second bird that Steele shot was the one that struck me as it tried to vacate the area. The impact was such that it knocked me out of the tree and dazed the hefty bird. Before the plump hen could fully recover to fly or run away, Johnny finished her off with a load of lead shot. That night both the Buchanan and McClintock families feasted on turkey.

CHAPTER 5

The 'Crick' Monster

Oil Creek was unlike any other stream in the region. The bank along the upper part of the creek was relatively flat and cluttered with fragments of slate-like rock, smooth polished stones, and massive gray boulders. Thick strands of poverty grass and carpets of delicate moss smothered the ground not covered in stone. The lower part of the meandering stream was encompassed by a steep earthen embankment where canes of elderberry, chokecherry and blackberry waved from side to side in the persistent but gentle breeze. Oil Creek was much larger than the other coldwater tributaries in the region. Cherry Run was crystal clear and known for its abundance of wild trout, yet it was a only ten yards across at its widest point. Skunk Run got its name from the pungent skunk cabbage that grew along its banks; it to was only a few yards wide. Cherry Tree Run was a swift little brook that gushed into the creek above the McClintock farm. It was nearly identical to the former in both size and clarity.

Oil Creek was more than a hundred yards wide at some points, and though the average depth was only about three feet, there were several deep pools within the three mile stretch that veered through our little valley. In most parts of the country, Oil Creek would probably be classified as a river, however we referred to it as 'the crick'.

My favorite fishing hole was a large, deep pool located just below the Rynd Farm. Nearly fifty feet in diameter and over ten feet deep, the abyss was full of bass and bullhead catfish. I visited the hole about once a week and was often rewarded with a creel of tasty fish.

On a hot summer day in '54, Sarah Rynd and Permelia Steele were wading in the shallows near the hole while searching for colorful, polished stones. Sarah spotted a turquoise-colored one in the current at the edge of the pool and plunged into the water to retrieve it. Upon retrieving the prize from the creek bed and regaining her feet, she observed something unusual floating on top the water at the far side of the murky, green depths. She alerted Permi and when the girls moved in for a closer look, their frantic screams echoed throughout the valley corridor. They escaped to shore and dashed to the Rynd Farmhouse to hide. They related their terrifying encounter to their siblings, and within a few days the chilling tale reached everyone in the community.

A beast with a large flat head, eyes as black as coal, and a mouthful of sharp serrated teeth was lurking in the depths of Oil Creek near Rynd Farm. Sarah described the creature as being the same color as mud with darkened stripes, like those of a tiger, across its smooth back. Permi said that its body was also flat with folds of thick, wrinkled skin hanging along the underside. Its legs were powerful and its toes were fitted with long, sharp talons. The long tail was flat and rudder-like.

The most incredible part, however, was that both girls declared that the creature was as long as a man is tall. Both were clearly frightened by the encounter and referred to it as the bloodthirsty 'crick' monster.

When word got out, most of the children vowed to never set foot in the creek again until the beast was killed. I must admit that when I first heard the news, I was uneasy about fishing in the area. I opted for another nice pool down the creek just below our property and found it nearly as productive.

When Johnny caught wind of the story he reasoned that the so-called beast was merely a snapping turtle or a muskrat, both of which were common inhabitants of Oil Creek. The girls, however, dismissed this as nonsense, so Johnny felt that it was our duty to hunt down and kill the hideous beast.

Johnny devised a plan and convinced me to assist him in executing it. We were going into battle against the Oil Creek Monster. Unfortunately, I wasn't informed of the specifics of the plan until after the fact. Johnny brought the big horse pistol that he had inherited from Mr. McClintock. The hefty piece was primed and loaded with a full charge of buckshot. He handed me a sharp, flint-tipped prod that was used for gigging fish. The spear was longer than I was tall. He also tucked into his waist band a leather pouch that reeked of something awful.

As we began our journey up the creek bank, little Eleanor Moffitt trailed behind. Johnny ordered her to go home, but she refused. She informed us that she was aware of our intentions and wanted to help. "That's the most stubborn, doggone girl I've ever known!" He shouted. When Johnny suggested that the serpent would probably eat her whole, she just shrugged her shoulders and claimed that she wasn't afraid of no monster. Johnny eventually let her tag along.

Once we reached the shallows near the hole, Johnny recited his plan. To my surprise, I would be the bait that would lure the beast into shooting range. Eleanor, who seemed to favor danger, expressed her disappointment when Johnny ordered her to stand on the bank as a spectator. He reckoned that she could alert us if the creature approached from some location other than the hole.

Johnny drew the pistol from his waist and waded into the creek. I had second thoughts as we started across the swift current of the shallows towards the depths ahead. I didn't like the idea of acting as a lure for whatever was out there. When I suggested that we revise the plan and use Ellie as the bait, Steele reasoned that the monster would much prefer a chunky fellow like me than a skinny lil' girl. He assured me that I'd be alright and reminded me of the time when he saved my butt from the rattlesnake.

We cautiously waded to the edge of the pool, where the water was now waist deep. I could see a shelf of rocks in front of me that looked like steps leading into the murky abyss below. Bream and goggle-eye were patrolling the layered shelf in search of minnows, nymphs, and tiny crustaceans. Johnny splashed his way to a point just above the hole where a boulder protruded above the surface of the water. With much difficulty, he climbed atop the slick, moss-covered mass and stood to his feet. "I got a good view from up here," he informed me as he placed the pistol under his armpit and reached for the leather pouch at his waist. Reaching into the pouch, he removed a handful of bloody muck and tossed the raunchy smelling chum into the current above me.

Johnny informed me that it was the entrails of a hog that Mr. McClintock had butchered a few days earlier. I watched as the pieces of tripe and intestine drifted along the current before sinking to the bottom of the creek near my feet. Steele figured that if the commotion of my kicking feet didn't attract the beast, than the smell of blood and guts would. Now the bloody aroma, along with my flailing legs and feet, was sure to attract the monster, and when it was about to make a meal of me, Johnny would unload his pistol on it. Holding the spear in a defensive position, I began dancing around, stirring the water. I kicked up rocks from the creek bottom and watched as crawdads darted in every direction, searching for another crevice to hide in. A half-hour turned into a hour, and still no monster. Just when we were about to give up, Johnny spotted something approaching from the far side of the hole. His eyes widened as he raised the big pistol into the air and cocked the hammer. "Good grief!" he uttered, scaring the crap out of me. "Hold steady Drew! It's comin' your way." I trembled in fear as I visualized a creature like an alligator grabbing hold of my legs and pulling me under. Now I had never seen a real-live alligator, but I had read about them and seen a picture of one in the school reader.

Johnny lowered the pistol towards the surface of the water and took careful aim as the slithering body continued across the water in my direction. The submerged back of the creature resembled that of an aquatic reptile. When the thing came uncomfortably near, I abandoned the spear, turned, and made a mad dash for shore. When I finally neared the bank, exhausted, Ellie helped me out.

We turned and watched as Johnny tucked the pistol into his waist band and lunged headfirst into the water. Moments later he emerged with a thrashing, three-foot serpent in his clutches. He struggled to carry the squirming creature ashore. "Are you crazy?" I hollered as he approached us.

The Oil Creek Monster was actually a mudpuppy, a big salamander common to the larger rivers and streams in Pennsylvania. This particular specimen was much larger than the average two-foot length.

Sarah and Permelia later confirmed that Johnny's new-found pet was indeed the beast they observed in the dark water below Rynd Farm. John W. Steele had conquered the mighty serpent and made the waters again safe for our recreation.

CHAPTER 6

The Bully

The fall of 1854 was a difficult one for the McClintock family. Johnny's sister contracted a virus and died several days later. The loss was almost too much for the young boy to bear. Permelia was two years his senior and the only blood relative he knew of. It was rumored that Johnny's parents had succumbed to an influenza outbreak when he was just an infant. Though Culbertson and Sarah McClintock were loving and caring foster parents, the boy couldn't help but feel abandoned in a young life so full of tragedy and grief. Shortly after Permelia's death, Johnny confided to me that the loss had opened a gaping hole in his soul. He couldn't understand why God would allow someone so beautiful to pass at such a tender age. Steele withdrew himself from me and the other local children for several weeks before Mrs. McClintock welcomed another member into their family.

Her name was Emily Scott. She was three years our senior and the prettiest girl who ever set foot in the Oil Creek valley. Emily was Mrs. McClintock's niece and was left behind when her mother contracted tuberculosis and had to move south to a more hospitable climate. Emily's presence appeared to relieve Johnny of some of the pain surrounding the loss of his sister.

Later that same winter, Culbertson McClintock purchased a new cookstove. A modern marvel, it was so large that Mr. McClintock had to build an extension onto their one-room log house. Johnny's excitement over the new additions (Emily and the stove) led to some bragging. My fabricated tales about Johnny whippin' that bear and snatching rattlesnakes with his teeth impressed our female classmates but began to test the nerves of some of the local boys.

One of those just happened to be the preacher's boy, Edgar Slentz Jr. He was the biggest boy in school and a bully who thrived on intimidating the other children. One day while class was in session at the little academy in Cherry Tree Township, Slentz overheard little Eleanor Moffitt repeating one of my tall Johnny tales to another girl. The sturdy lad adored Ellie and had a terrible disdain for Steele, so jealousy and pride began to fuel a nasty fire.

When Mrs. Crosby dismissed class at the end of the school day, Slentz rounded up two other local thugs and followed Johnny and me down the beaten path. The path was actually an old deer trail that meandered its way through the wooded plateau along the creek. A quarter-mile later the trail split into two directions. To the east it ended at the Rynd Farm, and two the west it traversed a steep hill before plummeting down onto the McClintock property.

As we approached a bend in the trail, Eleanor Moffitt stepped out from behind an ancient red oak. A look of desperation clouded her pretty face. "Johnny! Drew! Run!" she shouted as she focused on the forest behind us. About that time Slentz and his thugs came running up the trail. Slentz was consumed with anger and hostility raged across his face.

When Johnny realized that we were outnumbered and greatly overmatched, he grabbed Ellie by the wrist, turned, and hightailed it down the trail with me close behind. Now Steele was a swift and agile runner, and there's no doubt in my mind that he and Ellie would have outrun those bullies. However, I was another story. Pudgy, knock-kneed and flat footed, I was as swift as a fly in molasses. My nickname in grammar school was 'Mutton' because the children claimed that I was as clumsy as a newborn lamb.

I ran as hard as I could, but by the time we reached the bottom of Rynd Hill, one of the bullies had caught up with me. The big bully hit me so hard from behind that I toppled several feet down the embankment and landed face down at the edge of the creek. When I raised my aching head I was staring into the cold, black eyes of a huge crawdad. The angry crustacean raised its brawny claws and retreated into the swift current ahead. As I gathered myself up from the stony ground I turned and was overcome with fear when I saw all three boys standing above me. With clenched fists, Edgar Slentz began his descent down the embankment. "Look fellas! It's Steele's fat lil' sidekick," the bully shouted as he closed in. "What about Johnny?" one of the thugs asked. "We'll git him later. Let's send Buchanan back to him with a message," Slentz replied. "What kind of message?" the thug asked. "A black and blue one!" the preacher's boy answered while pounding his fist into his open left hand.

The anticipation of the pain I was about to endure made me quake in my shoes; but just then a voice rang out from somewhere on the hillside above us. "Leave him be! Come and get me you no-good bastards!" Steele was no longer in retreat, and was now hiding among a tall stand of beech and hickory. An evil grin came over Slentz's face. "I'll deal with you later," he said to me as he turned and proceeded back up the slope. I was relieved that my beating was going to be delayed.

"Steele! You no good braggart! I'm gonna find you and make mincemeat out of you!" Slentz's hostile voice rang out. "Find 'im boys!" he demanded as the threesome scattered into the forest. A few minutes later a boy's screams echoed through the darkening woods. One of the bullies came running out onto the trail with a large rat snake coiled around his head. Still screaming while attempting to unwrap the scaly critter, the frantic thug darted back towards the schoolhouse. "You coward!" Slentz hollered as serpent boy fled out of sight. "Keep searchin'. We'll find him!" Slentz ordered the remaining bully.

The bully climbed to the upper part of the ridge where he spotted a movement near a wagon-sized boulder. "I gotcha now!" he declared, confident that Steele was hiding behind the huge, moss-covered rock. As the bully began to shinny up the face of the slimy mass, he was startled by an eerie growl. When he reached the top he was greeted by a hideous sight. Face to face with a beast with a wolf's skull for a head and the body of a wildcat. The beast snarled, and vapor shot out from it's bony nostrils as rage illuminated its deeply sunken eyes. When the beast lunged forward, the bully tumbled back down the giant rock, regained his feet, and made a beeline for the schoolhouse. Slentz watched as the terrified boy dashed out of sight. "Doggone cowards," he mumbled to himself as he continued up the trail.

When Slentz reached the top of the ridge he found what he was looking for. Johnny was sitting atop the boulder removing the bleached skull of a gray wolf from his pet dog's head. The skin of a bobcat and a ball of twine sat on the ground below. "I gotcha now!" Slentz hollered as he confronted Steele. Weasel growled until Johnny shouted a command. Then the scruffy mutt hightailed it for the farm. Johnny stood up on the rock and jumped around, hollering at the top of his lungs. I had finally gotten up enough nerve to make my way up the trail to try to help my friend when, for the second time in a few short months, I had to witness the pitiful display. Johnny kept on a hootin' and a-hollerin' and the loud, profane exhibition was almost unbearable. A look of complete confusion came over Slentz' face. It was the same expression exhibited by the old bear the first time I witnessed the fanatical act.

Moments later, however, Slentz shook off his confusion and broke free from the temporary paralysis that had overcome him. He exercised his clenched fists and ordered Johnny down off the rock. Johnny ceased with the goofy escapade and ordered Eleanor to go home. Ellie stepped out from behind a big rock and stood her ground. "No, Johnny. I'm stayin' to help you whoop this big bully!" she replied. But Johnny demanded that she leave. Eleanor reluctantly made her way down the trail towards the schoolhouse.

The fisticuffs was on. I tried to jump in, but Johnny ordered me to stay back, for he wanted Slentz all to himself. Ellie ran back up the trail, and to our surprise, we watched as Johnny pummeled the much bigger boy. We cheered as Slentz collapsed to the ground while Johnny threw jabs and roundhouses like a prizefighter. When it was all over, Johnny sustained a swollen lip and some bloodied knuckles. Slentz was the recipient of a bloodied nose, two black eyes and a sore jaw. The bruised and bloodied bully headed for home while the victorious John Washington Steele was rewarded with a kiss from sweet Eleanor Moffitt.

CHAPTER 7

Emily Scott

One warm day in the following spring, I moseyed down to the creek to fish for some supper. The bass were spawning, and because of their aggressive behavior, they were easy to catch. There was a deep pool below my father's farm, and it was here that I tossed in my line. I hadn't been fishing for more than ten minutes when I heard a thud and felt a burning sensation on my rear end. I was afraid that I had just been bitten by a rattler. Suddenly a hand grasped me firmly over the mouth. Believing that I was about to be scalped by a Seneca warrior, I struggled to break free. "Shush," whispered my abductor. I was relieved to recognize the quiet voice as Johnny's. "I got sometin' to show ya," he added. "What did you hit me with?" I asked, a bit agitated about my sore rump. "A rock. I didn't mean to hit ya, just wanted to get your attention. Follow me, and keep quiet," he ordered as we proceeded down the creek bank.

Clueless, I followed him a good ways down the creek until we came to a bend just below modern-day Rouseville. We then crossed some shallow rapids and climbed a steep embankment on the opposite side. We cautiously followed a deer trail through an old, dried-up pond that was now a swamp smothered in cattail and skunk cabbage. I was hot and tired, and the swamp reeked of decomposing plant matter. Though I was curious about Johnny's discovery, I questioned if it was worth trudging through the awful smelling muck for. When he ordered me to proceed forward on bended knee, I decided that I'd had enough. Johnny actually got down and crawled several more feet before taking up a prone position behind a dense growth of elderberry bushes. He again motioned for me to advance, and then he turned to focus on something ahead. The loud croak of a bullfrog drowned out the sound of the peepers, and I figured that this was what Johnny wanted to show me. My curiosity finally got the best of me, so I trudged forward to his position. On the way I collected a couple of thorns in the palm of my hand. "This had better be worth it," I said, grimacing in pain as Johnny placed his index finger over his mouth to silence me. As I crawled up abreast of him he nodded his head in the opposite direction. "There she is." He sighed.

I peered through the bushes and realized that we were overlooking a small tributary of Oil Creek that I had yet to explore. The bank on the opposite side was a steep hillside covered in mountain laurel. A large run of spring water hurtled down over the face of the slope where it gushed into the creek below. The erosion from the falling water had created a delightful pool and the sight reminded me of a painting I once saw of the mighty falls in upper New York. It was a pleasant sight indeed, but was it worth getting filthy for? Just as I was about to question Johnny about the need for our stealth, I discovered what so fascinated him.

My jaw dropped when I saw the naked body of Emily Scott floating on her back in the center of the pool. She was bathing in the crystal—clear water and enjoying herself. She was unaware of our presence and we watched as she swam from one end of the pool to the other. Now I had met Emily on only two or three occasions, but like every other lad in the valley, I was awestruck by her appearance. She was beautiful. Her dark, flowing hair highlighted her bright, emerald-colored eyes. Her fair complexion was as perfect as that of a porcelain doll. I once overheard Sarah McClintock lecturing Emily about her beauty. The woman told her niece that such beauty was both a blessing and a curse. Emily would never lack the companionship of a man because of her looks, but for every good man there was a bad one lurking about. Mrs. McClintock feared that many men would come a-callin' in the future, and she prayed that her niece would choose the right one.

Johnny spoke very little of Emily. Though he was captivated by her beauty, his heart belonged to little Eleanor Moffitt. He'd never admit it, but Ellie was the perfect match for him. She was pretty but tough, witty but easy to get along with. Emily was more flamboyant in nature. She was years ahead of her time when it came to the mannerisms of young ladies. She was a dreamer who spoke her mind and often claimed that she would never be a servant to her future husband. Instead, she would be an equal partner in both his love and, more importantly, his wealth.

Johnny and I continued to watch as Emily eventually pulled herself out of the pool and up onto the creek bank. She recovered a bar of lye and lathered up her upper torso. Her perky breasts were well developed for a girl of fifteen and she possessed an hour-glass figure. Puberty struck as I watched Emily gently rub lather over her shapely bust. The glands in my mouth began to excrete rivers of saliva when she bent over to lather up those long, voluptuous legs before finishing at her perfectly smooth, pear-shaped rear end.

Moments later she plunged back into the pool, scattering soap suds across the water's rippling surface. Guilt overcame me as I reflected on what Sarah McClintock had said about beauty being a curse and attracting both good and bad men. Maybe I was bad, I thought, for being so fascinated with the first naked girl I'd ever seen. Just as I was about to convince myself that I was clearly in the wrong, Emily climbed back out of the pool and sat down in a sunny spot along the bank. She then laid back on the flat piece of ground and stretched out her gorgeous legs to absorb the warm rays of the noonday sun.

I couldn't take it anymore. There was an unusual sensation developing about my groin when I got 'up' and proceeded back across the swamp before scampering home. I don't even think Johnny noticed my departure.

Whether she was aware of it or not, Emily Scott was the focus of our attention when she visited the pool on a weekly basis during the remaining spring and summer of 1855. For the first time in my twelve years, fishing and exploring took a back seat to a girl.

CHAPTER 8

Weasel's Final Battle

One early afternoon after helping my father around the farm, I met up with Johnny at the creek below the Blood property. We were going to explore the mountaintop on the opposite side where several huge boulders, some as large as a house, lay scattered about. Johnny referred to the place as 'Big Rocks'. It was an unusually hot day, and Johnny's dog seemed to enjoy plunging into the cool water as we crossed to the other side. Weasel enjoyed the water so much that we had to coax him out.

As we climbed up the tall embankment, I was discouraged about what lay ahead. Before us was a steep incline, thick with scrub timber and mountain laurel. At the base of the mountain was a cliff face nearly forty feet in height. An ancient spring had cut a narrow gully into the bedrock outcropping, and this is where our journey began.

The raspy chorus of cicadas and crickets greeted us as we slowly trudged our way up the rocky slope before reaching the lush, green forest above. I didn't care much for heights, so I was somewhat relieved when we cleared the cliff and pressed forward into the steamy vegetation. The mountainside continued at a steep incline, and momentarily I stopped to wipe the sweat from my brow. Johnny and Weasel continued on until he eventually noticed my lagging behind and called for a brief halt.

A few minutes later Johnny urged me to move on, since there were another creek and a mountain to cross before reaching our intended destination. He speculated that it was a good hour-long hike. With a sigh of exhaustion I suggested that we abandon the journey and proceed back down to the creek. I reasoned that on such a hot day we might catch another glimpse of Emily bathing. Johnny shrugged it off, and proceeded up the slope with his rambunctious little dog leading the way. I mumbled a few choice words before continuing on.

A short while later we crested the hill and proceeded down the opposite side until we came upon a swift little stream known as Cherry Run. The icy-cold water of the brook was full of wild speckled trout. I found no better-tasting fish in the region than this native species. With olive-green flanks speckled with splotches of violet and gold and a bright orange belly, there wasn't a handsomer fish in the water.

We quenched our thirst before proceeding through a valley thick with red brush and thorn apple groves. We stopped for a few minutes to dine on some succulent blackberries that we picked from a massive bush located at the base of another hillside. With a belly full of sweet berries, I was ready to journey on. We trudged our way up another steep incline before reaching the top of a small mountain that now overlooks modern-day Rouseville. It was truly an impressive sight. Before us stood a dozen wagon-sized boulders, and on the crest of the hill sat three megaliths. One was larger that the McClintock farmhouse.

The dimples in the huge rock made for easy climbing, and though it was covered in moss, it was a dry, deeply rooted fungi that didn't give way under foot. It wasn't long before I was standing on top and peering down onto the forest floor, some thirty feet below. Johnny carried Weasel up with him and gently placed the dog down before strolling to the far end of the enormous slab of stone. "Come over here." He hollered while focusing on something in the distance. From this vantage point we could see over most of the thick foliage, across three miles of forest, and down onto the backside of my father's farm. We could also see much of the meandering Oil Creek as it appeared to slither like a giant snake through the valley.

"We're on top of the world!" Johnny cheered as he raised his clenched fists into the air above his head. "Thank you, God!" I shouted in my excitement over this new-found paradise. Then a commotion from behind caught our attention. Just ten feet away, a large rattler had been sunnin' itself on a rock shelf. The snake's tail was rattlin' something awful but to our relief, it was retreating. Weasel spotted the serpent and leaped forward where the brave little dog stood between us and the scaly critter. "Relax, Weasel. He's leaving," Johnny quietly reassured the dog. But the angry canine's leg muscles tensed and he growled. As the snake quickly retreated, thirty pounds of agitated dog followed. "Leav'em be, Weasel!" Johnny shouted, but the dog ignored his master's command. "Get back here," he hollered, but the dog ignored him.

As Johnny stepped forward to recover his dog, Weasel lunged at the retreating reptile. The snake slithered to the far edge of the boulder, where it coiled its four-foot long body in a defensive posture. The viper held its head high in the air and at the ready as both Weasel and Johnny approached. As Steele bent over to grasp the dog, the snake thrust forward, barely missing the boy's left shin. The angry viper struck again and this time Johnny had to jump backwards to avoid its fangs. In doing so, however, he lost his footing and landed on his rear end.

Enraged, Weasel lunged and grabbed hold of the snake just behind the head. The dog clamped its teeth onto the serpent and the reptile coiled its scaly body around the scruffy foe. Weasel viciously tore into the viper while the intertwined enemies rolled across the top of the big rock. Johnny quickly regained his feet and commanded his dog to let loose of the snake. Weasel was in a heated battle, and his sole intention was to kill the snake. In an act of desperation, Johnny dove forward to grab hold of Weasel as the dog-snake duo rolled towards the edge of the massive rock. He was too late.

The animals plummeted three stories below; the little dog gave out a yelp, and then there was silence. Johnny immediately climbed down the side of the boulder and dashed to the dog's side. Weasel was gasping for air as blood flowed from his mouth and nostrils. The poor dog had landed on a stone the size of a wagon wheel; the snake was mangled, but was attempting to slither away. Johnny crushed the serpent with his foot. Consumed with anger and hostility, Johnny picked up the dazed reptile and tossed it several feet against an old pin oak. The serpent piled up a lifeless heap at the base of the tree.

Young Steele focused on the dog, and tears welled in his eyes as he understood the gravity of his pet's condition. "I got to get him home to Aunt Sal. She can fix'em!" Johnny whimpered as I pushed my way down the rock and stood at his side. He gently gathered Weasel in his arms and cradled the little dog as we proceeded down into the valley. We followed Cherry Run through Henry Rouse's property and back down onto Oil Creek. By the time we reached my father's farm, Weasel's breathing was extremely labored. The dog was again gasping for air when we reached the McClintock farm.

Johnny dashed across the big flat below the farm, calling out for Mrs. McClintock in desperation. She heard his cries and stepped out the front door. Exhausted, I was nearly a hundred yards behind when Johnny desperately handed the struggling animal to her.

When I finally got too the house I could hear Johnny pleading with his adopted mother to save the dog's life. She tried to remain calm, but as she examined the animal the tone of her voice was sure grief. She told Johnny to make Weasel as comfortable as possible by laying him in a bed of straw in the barn. "Isn't there somethin' we can do for him?" Johnny cried out in desperation. The dog was bleeding from its nose and mouth and its abdomen was bloated. "He's busted up inside. Weasel's bleeding internally. Oh, Son. I wish there was something I could do." Her voice communicated her grief.

Johnny spent most of the evening in the barn with his beloved pet. Mrs. McClintock stayed with him. At last his faithful companion succumbed to his injuries and died what Johnny later deemed a 'Soldier's Death'. In the week following, Johnny escorted me to a grave on the hillside above the McClintock farm. Weasel's name was engraved on a melon-sized boulder. "Mr. McClintock did it for 'em." Johnny remarked about the nicely etched letters. In front of the stone was a pile of rattler tails, some big and some small. "There's twenty of 'em. Weasel never lost!" He proudly claimed. A moment later he wiped tears from his eyes.

TRANSITION

CHAPTER 9

Another Terrible Loss

The harvest of '55 had been an exceedingly generous one for the Farmers in the Oil Creek Valley. A mild spring and summer, along with hard work, made for a bountiful crop. Following the harvest, Mr. McClintock and his brother Hamilton finished the frame addition to the log house. The new addition was larger and contained separate living quarters, which Sarah McClintock felt necessary, since Emily was becoming a woman and needed her privacy. The old log structure was converted into a kitchen.

Winter arrived, and tragedy once again struck the McClintock household. Culbertson McClintock died at the age of 45. Everyone in the valley mourned the loss of such a wonderful and loving man. He had devoted his life to hard work and caring for his family, and was just as generous to his neighbors. Mr. McClintock could always be counted on when others in our little community were in need. He had invited Johnny, Permelia, and Emily into his home and loved and cared for them as if they were his own children. Though he didn't care much for church and attended only occasionally, he had no known demons, for he steered clear of liquor, gambling, and anything else that tempted men in those days. He walked the straight and narrow and was a pillar in our community.

As could be expected, Johnny suffered greatly from Mr. McClintock's death. For the second time in a year, he lost someone very dear to him. Culbertson McClintock had been a wonderful father to Johnny. He had taught the lad how to hunt and fish and respect nature. He had trained Johnny to become a fine marksman, and though he expected help around the farm, he always allotted the boy time to hunt, fish, and explore the surrounding countryside.

It was a long spell before Johnny returned to school at the Academy in Cherry Tree township. He eventually accepted his role as man of the house and the great burden that had been placed upon his broadening shoulders. With his determination, and Sarah McClintock's intelligence and hard work, the McClintock farm was in good hands.

I was saddened because by the spring of 1856, our childhood adventures had pretty much come to an end. Johnny took up the plow and had no reservations about being a farmer. The spring of that year also marked the end of my foolish dreams about Emily Scott becoming the future Mrs. Andrew Buchanan. A few days following her sixteenth birthday she married Richard Moffitt and moved to Dempseytown in Oakland township. Sadly, a few years later she died while giving birth.

CHAPTER 10

Drake's Well

In August of 1859 near Titusville, a Yankee named Drake drilled a well and pumped crude oil from the ground. In those days petroleum was collected as a substitute for coal in the production of kerosene and coal oil. Prior to Col. Drake's well, oil bubbled up from underground springs and floated down the creek hence the name "Oil Creek". Farmers used rags to skim the precious substance from the top of the water and applied it to lubricate wagon wheels and light torches. This laborious method produced about one barrel a year. Decades previously, the Seneca Indians dug pits along the banks of the creek. When the creek flooded during the following spring, the water filled the giant cat holes before being absorbed into the ground. The oil, however, remained, and was collected by the Indians for fires and medicinal purposes.

It wasn't long before Drake's well was producing 25 barrels a day. Once word got out, it spread like wildfire. Prospectors from all over the union began filtering into our serene, little valley. Men dressed in high boots and flannel shirts arrived on horseback and offered amazing sums of money to lease our land in search of the black gold.

With the influx of oil prospectors came a crowd of laborers who would work in the new oil trade. Carpenters and stonemasons arrived to clear the land before constructing derricks and pump houses. Teamsters were the hardy men who would transport barrels of oil via wagons to various shipping points along Oil Creek and the Allegheny River. Pilots navigated the turbulent creek while transporting the precious cargo on hastily-built rafts. Coopers opened shop and mass-produced wooden barrels to meet the demand of the new trade. The oil men arrived to make a fortune, and they were promptly joined by the merchants and saloon operators.

Boomtowns began to spring up everywhere—Titusville, Oleopolis, and Petroleum Center, to name just a few. When my family arrived in the Oil Creek Valley just a few years prior, Oil City, which sat at the confluence of Oil Creek and the Allegheny River, consisted of a mercantile, a blacksmith shop, a mill, and a few homes. Now it was a large and thriving community of fifteen hundred residents and the center of the new oil trade.

A drastic change came to our lives. Once dirt-poor, my father had barely enough property to support two or three leases. Yet the money advanced to him in royalties allowed for certain luxuries. Crafted furniture, elaborate paintings, and fancy renovations began to appear within our home.

The Oil Creek Valley was no longer the threshold of our universe, for parents now had the finances to send their children to college or private academies elsewhere. Of course, with wealth came temptation, and this often led to the downfall of good men.

I can still recall the time my father received his first bonus from the no. 2 well on our property. The lease operator handed him four-hundred dollars in cash, most of which he gave my mother to stash in a cubby. With fifty dollars remaining in hand, my father climbed aboard a horse and rode into Oil City. He told my mother that he would return before nightfall with a gift for her. The following morning he stumbled into the house reeking of stale tobacco and rotgut whiskey.

It was nearly a week before my mother spoke to him again.

CHAPTER 11

The New Oil Trade

By 1861 nearly everyone in the valley was involved in the new oil trade. Farming was no longer a livelihood, but a mere chore by means of which corn and beans supplemented diets rich in beef, lamb, and even seafood. A few residents, namely John Benninghoff and Henry Rouse, were becoming extremely wealthy from leasing their land. The oil prospectors fancied the flat land along the creek, and anyone owning a good amount of it was guaranteed at least a small fortune. The Culbertson McClintock property had several productive wells, but with all the money Sarah McClintock was raking in on the royalties, she continued to live a conservative lifestyle. She was, after all, a deeply religious woman who believed that money should not change one's convictions about God and family.

The wells on my father's farm were beginning to dry up, and it wasn't long before I had to take up a job as a teamster. I was eighteen when I began hauling oil, and by the time I had completed my first delivery to Oil City, I owned one of the foulest mouths in the region. It was all because of 'mud'. The hillsides surrounding the creek had been cleared of trees, for the timber was used to construct the derricks, pumphouses, and shanties that now cluttered the once serene countryside. The topsoil was no longer protected from erosion by the thick foliage of the trees, and the end result was mud, mud, and more mud. The creek was the color of coffee and the roads and trails that followed its course were virtual rivers of muck. One ruddy old teamster claimed to have lost a mule in a deep pool of mud. We later discovered that he lost the animal in a game of chance and didn't want to upset his wife. Another fellow who knew the couple claimed that she outweighed him by a hundred pounds.

Not long after I started hauling oil, I was headed to Titusville with a load of barrels when I met up with Johnny. It had been some time since we last spoke, and I discovered that he had just returned from Pittsburgh. Johnny told me that he was impressed with the Iron City and all of its luxuries. He stayed in a fine hotel and rode street cars while drinking expensive liquor and domestic beers, unlike the gut-wrenching corn mash whiskey we were accustomed to. He traveled aboard a luxurious steamboat and shopped in clothing stores that tailor-made suits and hats. The big city had certainly opened young John Steele's eyes to the world beyond our little valley. I admit that I was a bit envious, considering I'd never been to the city.

Johnny eventually took up the occupation of piloting, which suited him well. Navigating the creek on pond freshet days with hundreds of other boats loaded down with oil was a hazardous job indeed. The meandering waterway was full of sharp bends, rough currents, and undertows, and only a courageous man would task himself to pilot the hastily built flat boats.

Later in the year Johnny kept a promise by taking Eleanor Moffitt as his wife. Little Ellie was now a woman of eighteen, and she made a beautiful bride. In accordance with Mrs. McClintock's wishes, Johnny and his new wife took up residence at the McClintock farmhouse.

CHAPTER 12

Fire and Brimstone

Along with the wealth that followed the oil trade came danger. Carelessness around the flammable substance usually resulted in a pump house or derrick being burned to the ground. Natural gas often escaped from the earth during drilling, and it would ignite, blowing the wooden shanties to smithereens. Fortunately deaths were uncommon, at least until one April afternoon in 1861. On that fateful afternoon, the 'Little and Merrick' well located on our farm just below the Rouse property exploded and caught fire. Oil and gas shot up from the blazing well, climbing a hundred feet into the air. Above the pillar of flames loomed a rolling, black cloud of smoke. Balls of fire bolted across the surrounding landscape, igniting the few remaining tree tops. The horrible fire blazed for three days before my father, Johnny, and I, plus several spectators, were able to extinguish it with dirt and manure.

A derrick, pumphouse, and the Rouse barn had been incinerated. The real tragedy, however, was the loss of life. Nineteen people were killed. Some died from the explosion, while others succumbed to the burns they suffered during the blaze. Amongst the dead were the lease operator, Henry Rouse, several hired hands, and a dozen teamsters.

The loss of Rouse sent shockwaves through the valley. He was one of the patriarchs of our community. A retired merchant turned farmer and oil man, Henry Rouse and Hamilton McClintock were the founding fathers of what is today the prosperous towns of Rouseville and McClintockville. To this day, the explosion and fire at the well on my father's property remains the greatest tragedy ever to befall the Oil Creek Valley.

Yet another terrible accident occurred in May of the same year. A local teamster and his two young children were returning from Titusville with a load of provisions. Waitz road along Oil Creek was flooded, so the man had to direct his team up the steep incline known as Rynd Hill. With terrible difficulty the horses pulled the heavy wagon, laden with sacks of flour, grain, and a whole side of bacon, up the trail leading to the top of the hill. As the team crossed the crest of the hill, a dry, rotted harness snapped, causing one of the horses to break free. The remaining animal lost its footing in an oil spill created by a smashed barrel. The horse splashed onto its side into the muck, causing the wagon to career over the struggling animal before flipping end over end down across the steep hillside and crashing onto the banks of Cherry Tree Run. In the process, the two little boys were crushed under the weight of the vessel. Their father was thrown from the wagon, and he slammed head-first into an old pin oak. In less than a month we lost 22 people to fire and accidents.

For years afterwards, some locals reported seeing two small boys wandering the hills beyond the Rynd Farm. Some say that at night you can hear the apparitions calling out for their father. One gent claimed that early one evening while traveling along the same trail, he was actually approached by two boys in torn shirts and muddy britches. The boys asked him if he'd seen their father. When he replied in the negative and offered them a ride, they sadly turned and walked away, disappearing into the darkened forest. A doctor traveling along the same trail en route to Oil City claimed to have watched a wagon topple down over the hill in front of him. When he hastened to the bottom of the steep incline to investigate, he found no wagon, nor any other physical evidence to confirm his frightening observation.

CHAPTER 13

A Fallen Soldier

By 1863 the oil trade was in full swing in our once-secluded valley. The wells on my father's little farm had completely run dry, so I supplemented our dwindling income by transporting crude oil to Oil City. One late afternoon while traveling the road back from Oil City, I happened across a young fellow limping along the muddy highway. I could clearly see the difficulty in his gait. I halted the team and offered the stranger a ride. As he turned to face me, I recognized him as an old classmate.

James Miller resided on the farm just below Petroleum Center. There was a blank stare about his eyes, and he appeared to be focusing on something above and beyond me. I felt goose bumps as I realized that he was peering right through me. He became frightened and started back up the trail, so I tossed aside the reins and climbed down from the wagon. I maneuvered my way in front of the poor, hobbling soul as he struggled to escape me. "James! It's me. Andrew Buchanan. From the Academy in Cherry Tree." I did my best to reason with him. Slowly his senses returned.

"Drew." He muttered, clutching my arms to support his weak, emaciated frame. I offered him a ride and helped him onto the wagon, where he struggled into the buck-board seat. A large bandage was wrapped around his right thigh. The bleached linen was saturated in seeping blood and splattered mud from the trail.

Miller had recently arrived home after serving with the 56th Pennsylvanian Regiment under Maj. Gen. John Reynolds in the battle of Gettysburg. Several pieces of shrapnel from Confederate artillery had buried themselves deep in the private's thigh. Fortunately, no arteries were pierced by the iron shards. James's older brother Robert wasn't as lucky. A musket ball from enemy fire shattered his shin bone. Robert died while holding onto his younger sibling's hand as the surgeons attempted to amputate his lower leg.

The horrible battle lasted only three days, yet ten-thousand men were killed and another thirty-thousand were wounded. I soon realized that hopelessness owned young Miller's soul. The screams of dieing men in his head were very real, for the bloodshed in such a battle was overwhelming. The gruesome death of his beloved brother weighed heavily upon his youthful mind.

Though the War of Secession was often the topic of local conversation, the battles seemed a world away. The oil trade and its industrious servants didn't have much time for the conflict. Accumulating wealth led to greed, and greed often removed many from the reality of the world beyond our prosperous, little region.

I gave Miller a ride home. Sadly, it would be the last time I'd ever see him alive. A few weeks after my chance encounter with the young veteran, he died from an infection. The American Civil War had taken two of our finest and most dedicated young men. I regularly visit their gravesite in the peaceful little cemetery just beyond the Miller farm.

CHAPTER 14

The Prize Fight

Johnny also attended Miller's funeral. When I spoke with Johnny afterwards, he told me that Wright's mercantile was sponsoring a prize fight on the following afternoon. The bout was between champion Ben Hogan and some local ruffian. I had never witnessed a fight involving a professional before, so I was eager to attend. That is, until I discovered that the brawl was to take place in the city square at Petroleum Center.

Petroleum Center was an oil boomtown situated four miles up the creek from my father's farm. The town had yet to establish a government, and its only law was a rogue sheriff and a drunkard of a deputy. The "Center" was a vile, lawless place that had a complete disregard for decency. It was not safe for a man to walk the streets alone at night, for knife-wielding, club-toting thugs scoured the dark alleys for prey. The saloons were full of greedy oil men, drunken gamblers, and babbling lunatics hoping to score with a pretty hostess. The wickedness of the place rivaled any western mining camp or cow town that you would read about years later.

Along with the half-dozen saloons, the shantytown consisted of two banks, four hotels, several stores, an iron works, and a lumber mill that also supplied the place with caskets. There were a church and a red-light district. When I reminded Johnny of the dangers lurking in the town, he grinned while raising the red sash draped over his hip. He removed a short-barreled Colt's revolver. "Bought it yesterday. Down in Oil City," he said as he let me handle the gun. "It's a forty-four." I looked at my reflection in the finely polished brass trigger guard. Though I had hunted with a shotgun as a boy, I had never experienced a revolver, nor did I care to. Afraid that I might accidentally discharge the weapon, I carefully handed it back to Johnny. He eventually convinced me that we'd be alright if we just slipped into town for a couple of hours to watch the fight and drink a beer.

The following afternoon I met Johnny on the muddy trail along the creek just above the Rynd Farm. Johnny mentioned that his trip to Petroleum Center was against Ellie and Mrs. McClintock's wishes. I had been anxious to witness Ben Hogan fight, but I felt a bit deflated, since I regarded Sarah McClintock as the most intelligent human being in our valley, and trouble usually followed when a person disregarded her advice.

Several teamsters with fully loaded wagons passed us on the trail. A ruddy, little carpetbagger attempted to sell us some bottled liquor that he claimed was a cure-all. And a wretched thug eyeballed us with an alarming grin until Johnny lifted up the sash, exposing the butt of his revolver. On the trail about a mile below the "Center" we were amused to witness a collision between two flatboats containing full loads of oil barrels. The impact from the collision hurtled one of the pilots into the creek, and the other boat was smashed into splinters. Both pilots recovered and gave one another a tongue lashing of the most profane kind.

Twenty minutes later we arrived on the outskirts of town. I had visited the place earlier in the year to repair a wagon wheel, but I didn't stay long enough to really look it over. My mother had also warned me about the town. Johnny had also frequented the "Center" on business ventures, but Mrs. McClintock usually sent him to Oil City or Franklin for supplies.

Just like every other trail in the Oil Creek valley, Petroleum Center's main street was a sloppy excuse for a road. The mud and manure stretched some thirty yards between the elevated boardwalks that ran along the quarter-mile on either side of the hastily constructed buildings. The stench of the place was nearly unbearable. We trudged through the muck and climbed up onto the walk way in front of the Danforth House. The three-story hotel was bustling with patrons who were enjoying the pleasant, early October temperatures. We then passed the Lacy Saloon, which was relatively quiet, considering it was the most popular drinking establishment in town. A purple-draped brothel sat atop the two-story shanty. Several teamsters with wagonloads of oil rolled into town to refresh themselves with cold beer and catch the fight before continuing onto Oil City with their precious cargo.

As we proceeded towards the center of town I was approached by a beautiful hostess. She was employed by the Erie Saloon, and was looking to make a little extra money. As a single man, I was certainly taken with her astonishingly good looks. Not since Emily Scott had I seen a more attractive woman. She grabbed the crotch of my britches and gently squeezed while insisting that I needed her. For the sum of ten dollars, she was mine for an hour of pleasure. I was looking the devil in the eye when Johnny grabbed a hold of my arm and yanked me away. "Later!" he shouted as we continued down the walkway. I couldn't resist turning to catch a glimpse of my new-found love.

We continued to Wright's mercantile. Wright's was the largest store in town. In addition to dried goods and fresh meat, Billy Wright supplied the local population with the finest imported cigars and fresh tobacco from the Carolina's. A large sign was plastered on the big glass window. It promoted the fight between Hogan and George Croyle at three o'clock. More than fifty patrons crowded into the fancy store, most of whom were placing wagers on the afternoon's event.

Hogan was popular in Petroleum Center. Some considered him an outlaw who had swindled or intimidated his way into partial ownership of both the Tremont Hotel and the Erie Saloon and Brothel. Others felt that he was good for business. When Hogan arrived In Petroleum Center earlier in the year, he boasted about defeating over a hundred men in the ring and having never lost a fight. And no one had reason to doubt him. The walls of his saloon were covered with newspaper clippings from Pittsburgh, Buffalo, and Cleveland that declared him victorious in numerous bouts. There was also two large and imposing paintings of Hogan in a fighting stance.

George Croyle made Hogan look like a choirboy in regard to ruthlessness. Teamster turned robber, Croyle was the orneriest, no-good SOB in the region. He liked to drink, fight, steal, and kill. He was the ultimate bad-guy, and perfect for the prize fight.

Beyond the mercantile stood the jail. The Sheriff's office was a small wooden shanty built around two iron cages. The cells were barely large enough to house a man. On the walkway in front of the jail sat the deputy, a short, robust man who reeked of rotgut whiskey. His clammy, pale skin and sagging, tired eyes indicated he was suffering from a hangover. Next to the jail sat the office of George Prather. Prather was a petroleum banker and investor, and was regarded by many as the most knowledgeable oil man in the country. The sign on his door read, "Closed for Business—See you at the fight".

It was nearly three pm when Johnny and I arrived at the square in front of the Tremont. About a hundred people had gathered around the ring, while the catwalks along the hotel's three stories were crowded with spectators. Bets were still being placed, and Hogan was regarded as a four-to-one favorite. We pushed our way through the crowd and got as close to the ring as possible. A few minutes later, a middle-aged woman dressed in somewhat revealing attire climbed up into the ring. Her auburn hair and sparkling blue eyes, along with a large bosom, caught the attention of the menfolk. Her bright red, low-cut dress glistened in the sunlight. She was followed by an older gentleman who was dressed in a black suit and matching bow tie.

A few moments later, a mountain of a man stepped from the front door of the hotel and proceeded towards the ring. When he climbed up onto the ring the pretty lady threw herself into his arms and planted a kiss on his lips. I overheard one spectator telling another that the fine lady was known as French Kate.

Kate eventually released her hold on the fighter and stepped out of the ring. Hogan was surely an imposing figure. Weighing in at 225 pounds, his body was sculpted around a solid, six-foot frame. A handsome gent, Hogan swaggered in confidence and projected arrogance. Shirtless, he wore a pair of tight-fitting black canvas britches and matching knee-high, boots with no soles. The people cheered and acclaimed the champion as Hogan flexed his massive arms.

The cheers began to subside when the contender pushed aside the crowd and climbed into the ring. Many were in awe as an even bigger man stepped through the ropes into view. The challenger was a huge brute himself. At six feet, four inches, he outweighed the champion by at least thirty pounds. With a ruddy complexion, wide nose, and enormous forehead, he was the ugliest man, or beast, that I'd ever seen in my life. Croyle wasn't as muscular as Hogan, but he certainly was a fitting opponent.

The man in the suit had the combatants return to their respective corners. He then introduced the participants and informed the crowd that the fisticuffs would not end until one or both men were incapable of fighting on, or until one surrendered. Hogan drew cheers, while Croyle drew boos.

The bare-knuckled brawl lasted nearly thirty-minutes. Both Hogan and Croyle were suffering a beating, yet they continued on. Just when it looked like Hogan had the bigger man worn down, Croyle would let go of a punishing flurry to the champion's tender ribcage. Both fighters winced in pain, and at one point it appeared that Croyle would be the next champion. But Hogan never gave up.

Twenty-eight minutes into the fight Hogan landed a powerful roundhouse to Croyle's exaggerated jaw bone. The punch struck with such force that it completely spun the bigger man around and forced him to his knees. He slowly fell face-forward onto the canvas-covered surface. George Croyle was done.

The referee raised Hogan's left arm into the air and declared him the victor. Croyle eventually regained his feet and was helped out of the ring by a couple of teamsters. An exhausted and bruised Hogan would later declare that he had never fought anyone as tough as Croyle. When asked about a rematch, the Champion announced his retirement from the ring. He claimed that he was a businessman and wanted to retire while undefeated.

CHAPTER 15

Confrontation in the Boomtown

After the fight, Johnny and I returned to Wright's where we purchased a brick of tobacco. It was still rather early in the afternoon, and I suggested that we get a couple of beers before returning home. We stumbled into the Erie, which was choked with cigar smoke and babble from much of the crowd that had witnessed Hogan's victory. Two beers later, Ben Hogan walked into the saloon to the cheers of his fans. He held a large bronze trophy above his head to signify that he was still the champion.

A spectator from the crowd asked Hogan what he thought about Croyle. He responded, "I dislike the ugly SOB. But as much as I don't care for him. I'd hate to fight him again."

We wallowed in the Erie until there was but an hour of daylight left, and then I figured we'd better head home. We stumbled up the boardwalk and to the edge of town; then Johnny suggested we step into the Lacy Saloon for a nightcap. I was a bit reluctant but eventually agreed. Just like the Erie, the Lacy was thick with white smoke and boisterous patrons. A card game was in progress, and I recognized one of the players as George Croyle. His face was swollen from the beating he had sustained, but his demeanor was unchanged. Croyle had just lost another hand, and he demanded another bottle of whiskey from the barkeep. The bartender handed Croyle the bottle and informed him that it cost two dollars. Croyle backhanded the scrawny fellow with such force that he staggered back several feet, slamming into another patron. "It's on me!" the frightened man replied as he hurried back behind the bar.

Two beers later, darkness began to settle into the valley as the sun faded beyond the horizon. I was conversing with an old friend when Johnny decided that it was time to leave. I was engaged in such an interesting topic that I informed Johnny that I'd meet him out front in a few minutes.

Steele was waiting outside on the edge of the saloon's whitewashed porch when he felt a warm and unwelcome sensation running down his backside. He turned to see George Croyle, pants below the kness, urinating. Croyle was so drunk and his bladder so full that he couldn't make it to the outhouse that sat behind the saloon. Some speculated that since he was nearly a foot taller than Johnny he never saw Steele when he dropped his britches to relieve himself.

At about the same time, Ben Hogan was approaching the Lacy to congratulate the challenger on a well-fought match. When Steele realized that Croyle had just peed on him, he announced, "Piss on you!", drew back, and with all his might unloaded a lightning-fast roundhouse. When Johnny's fist connected with Croyle's forehead, the crash could be heard throughout the town. The impact caused the Giant to plummet onto the muddy highway some four feet below. With his pants down around his knees, Croyle attempted to recover. Dazed, he staggered to his feet before falling back into the muck. Croyle was unconscious.

Patrons laughed at the sight, and many cheered. Hogan had witnessed the whole thing. "Doggone, boy! It took me twenty-eight minutes and a beatin' to do that. What's your name?" he asked while looming over a half-naked and unresponsive George Croyle. Ben Hogan was now holding Johnny's right arm high in the air, declaring him the future champion.

CHAPTER 16

Mrs. McClintock's Death

Why some families are blessed with longevity and good health, while others suffer loss and grief is a question I'm sure will be answered soon as I am in the twilight of my life. Blessed I have been, for my father, mother and wife all lived to a ripe old age. All four of my children are healthy and have many children of their own.

In March of '64, shortly after the birth of Johnny's son, Sarah McClintock became another victim of tragedy surrounding the oil trade. Steele's beloved foster mother was severely burned in a stove fire while utilizing coal oil. On the following day, she succumbed to her injuries. Johnny and Eleanor were at her side the whole time, attempting to make her comfortable and praying for a miracle.

With Sarah's last breath, the cry of anguish could be heard throughout the valley. Johnny slammed open the farmhouse door and dashed out onto the grassy plateau above the creek and collapsed to his knees. He scolded and cursed Providence for having taken Mrs. McClintock. He buried his clenched fists into his tear-swollen eyes. Ellie ran to his side and took him into her arms in an attempt to comfort him.

Sarah McClintock believed in walking a straight and narrow path, and she helped many others along the way. A Presbyterian by faith, she could recite scripture as well as any old fire and brimstone preacher, and she rarely missed a Sunday service. An educated, hardworking woman, Mrs. McClintock was both a good teacher and excellent provider. She was also a forgiving soul who possessed a fine sense of humor. She rarely scolded Johnny for his constant practical joking, and often laughed at the tales of his escapades. On occasion she even became the target of a prank.

Sarah McClintock loved and treated all the local children as if they were her own. In fact, the youngsters addressed her as 'Aunt Sally', a title she graciously accepted.

Many evenings as a boy, I'd visit the McClintock farm where I'd be treated to tart, dried apples, crunchy roasted butternuts, and sweet berry preserves on freshly baked bread. Her pantry was always stocked with sweet things for the children. Aunt Sally was also a highly revered cook. The herbs that she grew in her little garden made for savory meals. Her mulligan stew and Sunday chicken and dumplings were the talk of the church socials. Some of the womenfolk within the congregation, including my own mother, tried to duplicate her recipes, but they rarely succeeded.

The passing of Sarah McClintock brought much grieving. Even with the energy and excitement surrounding the oil trade, the people within our community mourned for some time. I wept like a child, and was downcast long afterward.

WEALTH

CHAPTER 17

Johnny Inherits a Small Fortune

Following Mrs. McClintock's funeral service, Johnny escorted his wife, son and in-laws to the Moffitt home in Oakland Township. He then unhitched the team, climbed onto his favorite steed, and made the lonely journey back to the McClintock farm. Two hours later he was greeted by Mrs. McClintock's attorney and a local newspaper man. The short, bald-headed gent slapped dust from the sleeves of his tailor-made suit and adjusted the oversized spectacles that adorned his round, flushed face. He then recited the McClintock will, which listed John Washington Steele as the sole heir. After informing the weeping young man of his inheritance, the threesome proceeded into Mrs. McClintock's bedroom. A safe sat in the far corner of the room. It was partially concealed by a quilt draped over it.

The attorney kneeled and unlocked the heavy door. He removed some papers and a large bundle of cash from the cast iron box. "Mrs. McClintock was saving for your future," the little man remarked as he handed Johnny the deed to the property and the wad of money. "She was indeed a fine woman," he added as he stood up. Steele had not only inherited the farm and the thousand dollar-a-day royalties from the leases, but twenty-five thousand dollars in cash.

Tears streaked down across his cheeks as he kneeled to return the deed and money to the safe. "I am deeply sorry for your loss, Mr. Steele," the lawyer declared as Johnny closed the door. "My fee for reading the will is one thousand dollars. You can pay me now!" Steele hesitated. "Where's your sympathy now, you little parasite?" He mumbled under his breath. "What's that you say?" The clueless lawyer asked. Johnny did not repeat himself. Instead, he handed the greedy man his money and ordered both men to leave. The newspaper man was fumbling with a pencil and a small pad of paper as Johnny chased them out the door. "Half a million. Yeah, a half million sounds better," the journalist mentioned to the attorney while climbing onto the wagon. The frightened lawyer frantically whipped his team up the trail.

Johnny returned to the safe and removed a couple of bills from the wad of money. He crammed the cash into the front pocket of his best Sunday britches. He slammed home the safe door and walked out of the farmhouse and across the grassy plateau until he reached a massive stump that had once been a giant oak. The ancient tree had been cut down by Culbertson McClintock nearly twenty years earlier while clearing the land for cultivation. The roots were so thick, and the trunk so heavy, that no number of men, oxen, or horses could budge it. Johnny regarded this as the only battle Mr. McClintock ever lost, other than the influenza which ended his life. In fact, he had grown an admiration for the rotting relic. Johnny reckoned that the old tree had endured much pain, and yet refused to give up its ground. I think that subconsciously he likened it to himself. The grieving young man took a seat on the enormous stump.

It was Sunday, and the only day of the week that the wonderful sounds of nature weren't blotted out by the mechanical pounding of the steam engine pumps that powered the drilling rigs. The trails were free from the loud, profane utterances of the teamsters maneuvering through the mud while transporting their precious cargo. The icy rapids of the creek were free of riverboat pilots and their hastily built rafts.

Johnny peered into the sky and watched as puffy, gray thunderheads rolled in from the west. As the sky darkened, thunder rumbled in the distance and Johnny's life flashed before his eyes. He had stepped back into the past and was overcome with the memories of his childhood. He gazed at a stretch of creek and visualized Culbertson McClintock teaching a little boy to fish. Permelia was wading in the shallows nearby, searching for fancy-colored stones. He saw the excitement in her face when she recovered a turquoise-colored rock and splashed towards the fishermen, anxious to show them her find. Sarah McClintock walked along the creek bank toting a picnic basket containing a jug of fresh cider, ham sandwiches, and fresh-baked apple muffins. Permelia polished the brilliant stone with her skirt and presented it to Mrs. McClintock as a gift. The gracious woman marveled at the vividly colored rock before gathering Permi in her arms and hugging her tightly.

The family then gathered at a flat, grassy spot along the creek bank to the refreshment of supper and cider. Johnny could hear their voices within the frigid, churning water. Permelia's dainty giggles and Sarah McClintock's soothing voice radiated from the turbulence below. While the family gathered their belongings, Johnny playfully climbed onto Culbertson McClintock's back and was treated to a piggy-back ride to the farm.

With another loud clap of thunder, Johnny lost sight of his vision. The swollen creek was barren, and the voices were swallowed in the churning rapids below.

CHAPTER 18

A Fortune Won and Lost

A couple of months after Mrs. McClintock's funeral, Ellie became ill. A doctor suggested a change of scenery. Therefore, Johnny began making arrangements to move his little family to Philadelphia. He had heard many good things about the Quaker City, and Eleanor had relatives residing there, some of whom were prominent citizens.

One morning Steele rode into Franklin to consult with an attorney about the business affairs of the farm. He also hired an agent to look after the property while he was away. The greedy attorney's advice cost Johnny several hundred dollars and his agent requested five hundred more in advance.

Johnny was eager to leave the Oil Creek Valley with all the sad memories and exchange it for the excitement of the big city. But just prior to his family's departure, one of the men leasing a portion of the farm struck black gold. A gusher known as the 'Hammond Well' began producing three hundred barrels a day. In the days of the steam engine pump and boiler, three hundred barrels a day was unheard of. With the 'Lone Star Well' filling nearly two hundred a day, Johnny's income from royalties was about to swell beyond belief.

It didn't take long for word to get out about the Hammond Well and Steele's imminent fortune. The local newspapers picked up the story and within days, big city papers like those in New York and Pittsburgh were writing about the gusher. The paper in Oil City had previously reported that Steele inherited five hundred thousand dollars in cash when Mrs. McClintock died. Now it was labeling him as "The Oil Prince," and it wasn't long before other local papers addressed him with the same title.

Johnny began receiving mail by the sackloads. Ladies young and old, apparently unaware that he was already taken, wanted his hand in marriage. Others requested money for dresses and jewelry, often offering themselves in return.

Shortly after the Hammond Well struck gold, a man by the name of Wickham arrived at the farm. He was riding in an elaborate gold-colored carriage and was dressed in a fine European made suit. He haled from New York City and was partial owner of the Wickham and Jones Investment Firm, which was scrolled in black letters on the door of the carriage. The man was interested in purchasing Steele's one-eighth royalty right to the Hammond. When Mr.Wickham tendered offers, Johnny marveled over the carriage.

Johnny eventually agreed to sell his share for one-hundred thousand dollars plus the carriage. Arrangements were made, and Steele agreed to meet Wickham in Oil City on the following Monday morning to sign the necessary paperwork. Mr. Wickham would also turn over the carriage to Johnny, minus the Firm's logo.

On Sunday the well stopped flowing. It became flooded with creek water, and a fortune slipped through Johnny's fingers. By the time the bad news reached Oil City, the paper had already printed the story that the Hammond had made Steele a millionare.

CHAPTER 19

Philadelphia

Philadelphia was an elegant city at that time (1860's), for buildings constructed of brick and street lamps fueled by kerosene adorned its cobblestone streets. Fancy eateries, exquisite hotels, and dozens of shops lined the Quaker City's main strip. Street sweepers armed with straw brooms and tin pans kept the avenues clean by collecting and disposing of rubbish and horse manure. Burly policemen toting billy clubs walked their beat and at night hollered the time at the top of each hour. Union soldiers frequented the place; most of them were on their way south to fight in the great war being waged.

Drinking establishments, gambling halls, and brothels were common in big cities and Philadelphia was no exception, regardless of its nickname. The city even had its own race track.

Johnny and his family moved into a nice cottage on the outskirts of town. While Ellie healed and cared for their son, Johnny played, and play hard he did. With a seemingly endless amount of money flowing into an already large bank account, young Steele felt no need to rein in his spending. For the time being, his wife and child were well provided for, and saving money was low on the list of priorities. Having already lost most of his loved ones, plus a fortune when the Hammond Well flooded, Johnny was going to live in, and for, the moment.

During his relocation to Philadelphia, Johnny had run across a fellow named Seth Slocum. Slocum haled from Erie, and was the eldest son of a very prominent family. He frequented places like Buffalo and Pittsburgh and claimed that he knew Philadelphia like the back of his hand. A handsome gent, he possessed a smooth tongue. His confidence proceeded him so that many considered him downright arrogant. Seth Slocum was an insidious sort and showed few signs of possessing a conscience. Some considered him the Devil, but most people were drawn to this free spirit. One of those unfortunate souls was John Washington Steele.

Slocum was in need of a job, and Johnny needed guidance in his new venue. There-fore, he hired the dashing young man as his assistant. He agreed to pay his new friend a decent salary and cover all expenses incurred in their partner-ship.

Shortly after forming the partnership, Johnny's son contracted smallpox. Banished from his house by the quarantine, the devastated young father took up residence at a local hotel. Having been exposed to so much death in his young life, he was anticipating the worst. Yet Oscar made a full recovery, and shortly thereafter Ellie conquered her illness also.

By October Mrs. Steele had had enough of big-city living. She missed her family and the solitude of the farm. She also convinced herself that the city was no place to raise a young one. Though they had a vested interest in Philadel-phia, Johnny escorted his family back to the Moffitt Farm in Dempseytown. After checking on the affairs of the McClintock Farm, and against Ellie's wishes, Johnny returned to Philadelphia to see his investments through. He assured his wife that he would return for good in late November. Upon his return to Philadelphia, the Devil was waiting for him at the stage depot.

CHAPTER 20

The Philadelphia Career

Johnny always had a passion for horses, and upon his return to Philadelphia, his man Slocum persuaded him into purchasing a thoroughbred. It took only three pints of beer and some reassurance from the breeder for young Steele to commit a princely sum to own a racehorse. "We bought ourselves a champion!" Slocum declared as he ordered up another round of drinks. The threesome then traveled to Fairmont Park to revel over Johnny's grand investment. It was a handsome animal, indeed, and it didn't take long for Johnny to find a rider. A large down payment secured a jockey and a trainer, and it was agreed that the horse would be ready for the following Sunday's race.

Slocum's influence on young John W. Steele was becoming more apparent by the day. One morning after a long night of carousing, Slocum felt it necessary that the partnership purchase new duds. They strolled into a fancy clothing shop and had the tailor fashion two suits of identical design. The suits would be made of gaudy materials, and would include matching crimson silk shirts and yellow neckties. Slocum also talked Johnny into purchasing top hats and elaborate gold canes. Diamond pendants and gold cuff links would adorn the flamboyant outfits.

Dressed in his new attire, Johnny was skeptical as he looked himself over in a full-length mirror. He remarked that he felt uneasy about parading around town in such a getup. The confident Slocum convinced Steele that there was nothing to fear. He told Johnny that the townspeople would recognize them as the influential, upper-class citizens that they were. "We'll land in jail before nightfall," the doubting young man remarked. Against his better judgment the twosome started their trek around town. The townspeople gawked and patrons made unfavorable remarks under their breath as the brightly colored twosome strolled down the streets. "Look at the plumage on those birds!" a drunken soldier hollered, and half of his company broke out into laughter. A streetcar driver caught a glimpse of the pair, and awestruck by the spectacle, nearly ran his team of horses into a group of pedestrians. A policeman observed what was taking place and arrested both men for disturbing the peace.

Later on that afternoon, a fuming John Steele and his assistant were brought before the local magistrate. The charges were dismissed, provided that both men agreed not to wear the suits in public again.

Johnny and Slocum then visited a local tavern, where they indulged in spirits to celebrate their release from incarceration.

On the following Sunday, Steele's horse faired miserably at Fairmont Park. In fact, over the course of three weeks of racing, the horse never placed better than fourth. Johnny fired the jockey and trainer and demoted the animal to the team that pulled his carriage.

CHAPTER 21

The Philadelphia Career

Johnny was already living the high life when Slocum introduced him to the theater. Johnny was so overwhelmed with this kind of entertainment that the young entrepreneur invested in a theatrical group. The Skiff and Gaylord Minstrels were struggling financially, but Steele was so impressed with the band and its core of actors, comedians, and female impersonators that he purchased a half interest. He also provided the group with five-thousand dollars for new costumes, stage props, and posters. One of the promotional posters even bore a picture of Johnny and Seth Slocum in the upper right-hand corner.

To be closer to his investment, and on Slocum's advice, Steele moved out of the cottage and rented two rooms at the Continental Hotel. The rooms were actually converted into luxury suites to appease Slocum's appetite for expensive luxury.

Meanwhile, Ellie had been sending telegrams to Philadelphia in an attempt to persuade her husband to return, and to make him aware of the affairs on the farm. Johnny responded only to the initial telegram, and told his wife that he had to find a buyer for the cottage. He reassured her that he would be home within a few weeks.

The theatrical group was gearing up for a tour of four cities, and Johnny and his business partner accompanied them to Utica, New York and New York City. It was reported that Johnny covered the expenses of all twenty-plus members of the Skiff and Gaylord Minstrels. They stayed in the finest hotels and experienced the luxury of fine dining, and they consumed royal amounts of bourbon and wine. Upon his return to Philadelphia, Johnny was reported to have spent twenty-five thousand dollars on the road trip.

There was also a rumor circulating that on one afternoon, during a drunken stupor, Johnny purchased the Continental for a day. Apparently it took some persuasion, but Slocum convinced the hotel's proprietor to lease the fancy place for a generous price. After closing the deal, Johnny and Slocum sponsored an enormous banquet and invited many guests. The menu included fresh seafood, a whole roasted hog, bushels of boiled corn on the cob, and several cases of champagne and French cognac. Slocum visited the Fox Playhouse and hired several beautiful dance-hall girls to work as hostesses for the festive event. A comedian was also paid an outrageous sum to entertain the guests.

Johnny and Slocum sat in plush chairs positioned at the front of the dining room. A pretty blonde with gorgeous, long legs stretched across Slocum's lap while sipping on a glass of pink champagne. During a lull in the entertainment one of the guests requested to make a toast. The inebriated fellow raised his glass into the air and suggested that John W. Steele be elected President. The cheerful crowd raised their glasses to toast his nomination. Then they requested that Johnny make a speech. Steele staggered to his feet and reassured his happy guests that Abram Lincoln was doing a fine job.

The party lasted into the wee hours before Johnny, Slocum and some of the girls stumbled up to his room to continue the revelry. The laughing, drinking, and carousing lasted until dawn.

CHAPTER 22

The Philadelphia Career

Someone was pounding on the door. For the moment, Johnny was convinced that the annoying ruckus was only the throbbing pain inside his head. His mouth was dry and gritty, and he reeked of stale whiskey. He felt the warmth of another body pressed against his backside as he pushed himself off the plush sofa. In the darkened room he could barely make out the busty outline of a woman.

"Master Steele! You's in dare?" the Negro bellhop hollered from behind the hotel room door. Johnny stumbled to his feet and staggered across the room. When he opened the door, a burst of sunlight from the large window across the hall exploded into the darkness, nearly knocking the semi-conscious young man to the floor. Johnny held onto the door frame for support while shielding his eyes with his forearm. Behind the little Bellhop stood the shadowed figure of William Wickham.

Johnny stepped into the corridor, and in a few moments his eyes came into focus on the unusual grin that dominated Wickham's face. Dressed in an expensive suit crafted in Paris, the middle-aged man eyeballed Johnny's attire. Steele then realized what was creating so much delight for Wickham's usual 'I-mean-business' personality. The younger man looked down and discovered that he was wearing a scarlet, silk skirt. Embarrassed, Steele awkwardly explained to Wickham that the dress belonged to a dance-hall girl and that it was just part of a prank. The older man glanced at Steele's hairy legs and snickered, "Mr. Steele, when you're done with your prank, I'd like to discuss business."

"Mr. Wickham, I'm really not interested in any business dealings right now," Steele remarked. "Get dressed boy. I've got a proposition you can't refuse!" Figuring that Wickham had traveled all the way from New York City, Johnny agreed to meet him in the hotel's dining room at the top of the hour.

Johnny returned to his room, where he went to the window and pushed aside the drapes. Sunlight partially illuminated the room. A snoring Seth Slocum was sprawled across Johnny's bed. Beside him was a woman whose face was concealed by her matted, auburn hair. A quilt covered their bodies.

Johnny felt nauseated, for the room reeked of whiskey and cheap perfume. He sat down on the sofa and examined the girl who had been his bed partner. Her tangled blonde hair was swept aside revealing the pretty face of a woman in her early twenties. Her voluptuous body exhibited more curves than the Oil Creek valley and her legs were also shapely, typical of a dancing girl. Observing that she was partially naked, a terrible sensation overcame Johnny. Guilt festered in his mind as he thought about his wife so far away. Ellie was as pretty as any girl in Philadelphia, and the sweetest woman he'd ever known. "How could I have betrayed her like this?" He mumbled to himself. He felt like a cheater, and disliked himself intensely.

The evidence was clear. Slocum had set Johnny up with the pretty girl. She was wearing Johnny's undershirt and he was wearing her dress. Yet Johnny could not recall having actually been with the pretty girl. Of course, liquor was good at helping him forget things. Johnny remembered getting drunk, and vaguely recalled parading around the hotel room in the dress while Slocum and the girls laughed so hard they were in tears. But how did he end up with the girl on the huge chair? And how could any man resist such a fine woman? The guilt became too much for him to bear. He shook the pretty young woman to wake her. Eventually she rolled over and insisted that Johnny let her go back to sleep. Trying not to fixate on her fine body, Steele simply asked, "Did we?" Fortunately the girl was as bright as she was attractive. She slowly opened her gorgeous blue eyes and looked at Johnny. "You don't remember?" she asked. Some what ashamed, Johnny replied, "No. Whiskey makes me forget things." She closed her eyes and rolled back over. "All you talked about was your sweet little Ellie. And then you fell asleep before you could get into trouble. Why couldn't you be like your partner Slickum?" She remarked before attempting to fall back asleep. "That's Slocum." Johnny replied, relieved that he didn't commit the deed.

It was nearly eleven o'clock when Johnny and his hangover met with Wickham in the fancy dining room. The businessman was finishing a cup of coffee laced with brandy. Johnny was wearing his best Sunday suit. "What, no dress?" Wickham snickered before his expression became more serious in nature. "This is a beautiful hotel. Satin, oak floors, chandeliers crafted of polished German silver and gold. European drapes, and carpets from the orient. I'm in the wrong business, Mr.Steele."

"Sit down young man." Wickham demanded. "Can I buy you lunch?" he added. Still sick to his stomach from the overnight frolicking and whiskey, Johnny declined. He then asked Wickham about the reason for the meeting. Wickham quickly got to the point. He wanted to purchase the McClintock farm outright. He felt that he could make the farm more profitable with certain refinements—ones that only a seasoned businessman like him could provide. Johnny was not impressed. The farm was providing him with a steady income; besides, the memories of his family and his boyhood were to difficult to part with. Wickham raised the offer to one million dollars. Mouth agape, Johnny repeated back to him, "You said one million dollars?" "That I did, Mr. Steele," Wickham smiled. "Of course, there's a small problem concerning the deed. But I think we can hash it out in due time," he added.

Overwhelmed, Johnny got up from the table. "Can I think about it for a while?" Wickham added, "Mr. Steele, do you realize for that kind of money, you could own a dozen hotels as grand as this one?" Johnny nodded his head. "It's a generous offer. But I need to consult with my assistant." Steele replied. "Okay, Mr. Steele. I'm stayin' in room 307. I won't be leavin' until tomorrow evening."

CHAPTER 23

The Philadelphia Career

After Mrs. Steele's return from Philadelphia, I moved to Franklin, where I worked as a cooper for a local barrel manufacturer. Franklin was a sprawling community situated along the banks of the Allegheny River. Eight miles due west of Oil City, we were somewhat removed from the hustle and bustle of the oil trade. On occasion a barge loaded down with barrels of crude would become stuck on a sand bar while transporting the precious substance to Pittsburgh. The profanities uttered by the river men involved in such an incident equaled, or even surpassed, those of the pilots on Oil Creek.

During my employment with the Weston Barrel Works, I met and fell in love with my foreman's daughter. Amelia was a fine young lady and a dandy cook. She took an instant liking to me, and within a few weeks, and with her Father's blessing, we agreed to be married. When Eleanor Steele learned of my good news, she caught the first stage to Franklin and visited me at my new residence. She was happy for me. I requested her and Johnny's presence during the ceremony.

On the following morning Mrs. Steele had a telegram dispatched to Johnny in Philadelphia. By week's end she had not received a response, so she sent a second telegram. Again, no reply.

On December 20th 1864, I was married. Several people attended the ceremony, including our parents and Eleanor Steele. Finally, a week following my wedding day, Eleanor received a telegram from Johnny informing her of Wickham's offer to purchase the McClintock farm. Ellie responded by telling him of my getting hitched and the necessity of him returning home to Dempseytown to be with his wife and baby boy. She didn't care about any more business transactions concerning the farm.

Johnny's final reply noted that he had not received any telegrams prior to the wedding. He insisted to Ellie that he surely would have been present had he known. Angered by such incompetence, he would take up the matter with the local telegraph operator. Johnny also assured her that he would be home very soon. He also forwarded a sealed envelope that contained a thousand-dollar bill. The money was a belated wedding gift for my new wife and me.

CHAPTER 24

The Philadelphia Career

On the following morning Johnny and Seth Slocum reported to William Wickham's hotel room, where they were greeted by Wickham and his business associate. Curious about Slocum's affiliation, the seasoned businessman (Wickham) didn't seem to care for his company. Johnny convinced the aging entrepreneur that Slocum was his agent and was present only to act as counsel and as a credible witness on his behalf.

The four men sat at a thick, cherry table located in the center of the luxurious suite. Paperwork consisting of deeds and bank drafts was scattered about the finely varnished surface. After lighting a cigar and taking a couple of puffs, Wickham went to work. He pointed out a problem concerning the McClintock property deed. The original deed as conceived by Culbertson McClintock himself, listed his older brother, Hamilton McClintock, as the benefactor of several acres of land. The land was located on the extreme southern end of the property.

Mr. Wickham had done his homework. Johnny was aware that his foster Uncle owned 'the bottom seven', as they referred to it. Hamilton McClintock, inherited a mountain from his father. Unfortunately, there was very little level ground to grow crops. The property that his younger brother, Culbertson, had inherited was not as vast, but most of it was flat, since it was situated along the banks of Oil Creek. Therefore, several years before his death, Mr. McClintock granted his older sibling the lower part of the farm to grow corn to feed his family. This portion of fertile ground equaled seven acres.

The revised version of the deed, as concocted by Sarah McClintock's Attorney, failed to mention Hamilton McClintock and the lower seven. The new deed listed Johnny as the sole beneficiary of the property. It was either an oversight on Sarah McClintock's part or an intentional error, for she never cared much for her husband's brother. Given her good nature and devout spirit, Johnny believed it was the former.

Wickham considered this a minor glitch and informed Johnny that he would purchase the entire farm for one million dollars, if the lower seven acres were included. He agreed to travel back to the Oil Creek valley and try to persuade Hamilton to give up his portion of the farm. If McClintock refused, Wickham and his counsel, would ride into Franklin and present the new deed and contract to a Venango County Judge, who just happened to be one of Wickham's close friends. The graying businessman was confident that if such action was necessary, a judgment would be brought against McClintock, resulting in his eviction from the property.

Johnny knew Hamilton McClintock would not sell out so easily. At the beginning of the oil boom, McClintock stopped growing corn and leased the lower seven to a couple of oil prospectors. He was collecting a small fortune in royalties from four productive wells. Wickham questioned young Steele's loyalty in regards to a possible eviction.

Just like his Foster Mother, Johnny never cared much for Hamilton McClintock. He was nothing like his younger brother. Hamilton was a stubborn, hot-tempered old man. He had a short fuse when it came to youngsters, and he never accepted Johnny or Permelia as part of the family. In fact Johnny, overheard Hamilton refer to them as 'bastard' children on more than one occasion. Now the old codger was the only thing standing in the way of a fortune.

Wickham remained confident about the situation and provided Johnny an option.

The Businessman offered Steele thirty-five thousand dollars in cash to take control of the McClintock Farm, minus the lower seven. This money would be considered a down payment until the Hamilton McClintock problem was resolved. Then Wickham would begin paying off the million dollars in huge lump sums. Mr. Wickham's associate removed a contract from the pile of paperwork and laid it in front of a nervous and somewhat reluctant John W. Steele.

"Thirty-five thousand, up front! Sign it, Johnny!" An anxious Seth Slocum urged. Wickham turned to Johnny's wide-eyed, exuberant partner. "Listen to your friend, Mr. Steele. It's an offer you can't refuse." Wickham's associate placed a brief case on the table and opened it, revealing a dozen bundles of freshly printed banknotes. "Thirty-five thousand in cash money, boys!" The Businessman remarked. Johnny was still reluctant to sign. Slocum patted him on the back in reassurance. Steele thought it over. His new family was content residing on the Moffitt Farm, which was far removed from the oil trade. It was hard to relinquish all the wonderful boyhood memories, but there were more than enough sad ones also. He was growing tired of the hustle and bustle surrounding the oil boom, and he knew that Ellie felt the same. Johnny reached for the ink pen. "Where do I sign?"

CHAPTER 25

The Philadelphia Career

After signing the contract, the celebration began. The first order of business was to stash a portion of the enormous down payment in a local bank. Then the spending spree began. Johnny and his assistant traveled to the north side of Philadelphia to the Carriage Works Company. Steele ordered the most elaborate and expensive carriage on the market. Painted in black, with symbols of the oil region such as derricks and pump houses etched in gold, the five-thousand—dollar investment was to be delivered by week's end.

Slocum led Johnny to the finest jeweler in town, where they ordered gold watches and diamond necklaces for their family and friends. Johnny then suggested that they expand their wardrobe. So they went to a tailor of European descent and ordered several expensive suits designed to their specifications.

Later that evening, Johnny and his assistant arrived at a tavern in Philadelphia to unwind after a day of vigorous spending. Steele entertained the crowd by purchasing a drink for everyone in the house.

A crowd had gathered around a table in which a high-stakes card game was in progress. Four crafty fellows examined their cards and their opponents' faces as four-hundred dollars in cash in crumpled bills lay in the center of the hardwood table. "What you got?" an old, gray-haired fellow demanded. The handsome, thirty-something gent shifted his squinting eyes and was slow to reveal his hand. "Dammit, Brotherton! What you got?" the old man shouted. "Three whores (queens)!" he replied as he tossed his cards onto the table. "You are one lucky bastard," one player noted, for three of a kind usually succeeds only through a bluff.

George Brotherton was well known in Philadelphia. He had an uncanny ability to read cards and faces. A professional gambler, Brotherton made a comfortable living by playing cards and the faro games. An alluring gent, Brotherton's confidence in his game was superficial, and his personality was centered around humility. He was a mystery to both his gambling adversaries and those who befriended him.

Brotherton played one more hand and lost. As he got up to leave, one of the contestants asked if he was done. "Yup! I'm plum out of money!" he replied. As Brotherton got up from the table, a crumpled hundred-dollar bill was tossed into the pot. "Play one more hand!" Johnny ordered Brotherton. Confused, the gambler hesitated before sitting back down at the table. "It's your money, boy!" he replied as the dealer dealt the cards.

George Brotherton eventually won the hand and the four-hundred-dollar pot. He returned to Steele his hundred-dollar bill and bought him a glass of whiskey. They struck up a conversation and a friendship.

CHAPTER 26

The Philadelphia Career

The fancy brick building had once been a mercantile, and now sat dormant along Philadelphia's prestigious main strip. The owner was eager to sell the vacant building at a very reasonable price. Slocum and Brotherton convinced Johnny that billiards was the game of the future, and owning an establishment equipped with pool tables would increase his income several-fold.

Steele agreed to purchase the building for the sum of five thousand dollars as long as Brotherton agreed to manage the business. For the first few weeks, the attraction of the new game did generate a little business.

One morning while en route to Fairmount Park for the early races, Johnny observed a young gent striking an old steed with a leather glove at the stage depot. The horse was certainly an impressive animal, and Steele was dismayed by the owner's behavior. Johnny abruptly pulled his new carriage over and confronted the aggravated fellow. "I'll give you two hundred dollars for that horse!" Steele offered the angry young man. "Sir, this is the doggone orneriest, Godforsaken animal this side the Mississippi! If you want this crow bait for two hundred, he's yours!" Johnny handed the man two bills and tied the horse to the new carriage.

Seth Slocum questioned the purchase. He reminded Johnny of his last interest in a racing horse, which cost him several thousand dollars. "I know horses! This one's a winner!" Steele replied. Johnny acknowledged that he was inept at hiring a trainer and rider, so this time he would ride the horse himself.

Steele, Slocum and Brotherton placed a one-thousand-dollar bet on horse. At one-hundred and fifty pounds, Johnny was by far the biggest rider in the race. Steele pushed the ornery animal to its limits and the so-called barnyard heathen won the contest among a trio of thoroughbreds. He collected several hundred dollars from the victory.

Tragically, the animal contracted an infection from a shoofly bite and died a short while later. Johnny was crushed, for what appeared to be a sound investment was now lost and after weeks of nurturing and training, Steele had grown quite fond of the animal.

One afternoon, after the conclusion of another race, Johnny, Slocum, and Brotherton were occupying Steele's fancy new carriage while racing along Philadelphia's main strip. The clatter of the horse's hooves along the cobblestone street drew many a pedestrian's attention. One observer shouted, "That's Coal Oil Johnny and his gang!" A newspaperman overheard the comment and printed a story in the following day's edition.

CHAPTER 27

The Philadelphia Career

Slocum had allowed the specifics of the sale of the McClintock Farm and Johnny's pending fortune to leak out to a local man who ran a printing press. It wasn't long before a journalist caught wind of the story. "The Oil Prince" and "Coal Oil Johnny" and his new-found wealth were front-page news.

Johnny's popularity soared. Peasants, beggars, and even prominent citizens requested loans. Ladies practically threw themselves at his feet. Though he rejected their advances, Seth Slocum was always around to clean up. The immoral man was known to spend large amounts of money for the company of two or three girls and a night of frolicking. Most of the girls were employed by the Fox Theatre; on occasion, however, he'd stumble into Philadelphia's red light district while flashing hundred dollar bills.

Steele's generosity often provided help to the hard case that was truly in need of cash or provisions. When he got drunk, people often found it easy to separate him from his cash. Johnny's money was no longer any good, for the merchants, restaurant proprietors, and tavern owners extended him unlimited credit. Though he didn't really care for doing business that way, he knew that thieves and robbers lurked in the city's dark alleys. The credit relieved him of the burden of carrying large amounts of cash.

Johnny's reputation preceded him. He eventually became one of the most popular men in the Quaker City and people knew of him as far away as New York City and Washington. He and Slocum received invitations to fancy banquets, where most of Philadelphia's highly esteemed businessmen gathered to indulge in chit-chat, liquor, and women. The menu usually included fresh seafood, beef tenderloin, exotic desserts, and fine wines. It wasn't long before Johnny's shifty partner had everyone believing that Steele was the brightest young entrepreneur since Eli Whitney.

The story of Coal Oil Johnny and his exploits reached far beyond the local tabloids. Large publications in places like Buffalo, New York, and Washington were spreading fabricated tales. One column written by a Pittsburgh journalist claimed that as patron in a local tavern, Johnny was observed lighting a cigar with a hundred-dollar bill. Another claimed that Steele purchased a custom-made diamond watch for the sum of a thousand dollars and lost it later the same evening in a card game.

Regardless of what was being written, life was grand for the poor farm boy from the Oil Creek Valley. Johnny was aware that his days in the fabulous city were numbered. He knew that he had a responsibility to his wife and child, and guilt was beginning to set in. Yet the lure of the big city with its horse races, gambling halls, and nightlife was difficult to overcome. Liquor often distorted his better judgment, as did the cunning Seth Slocum.

In mid January 1865, Johnny received a disturbing telegram. Ellie felt that he had abandoned her and their son, and questioned why he had not responded to her letters and telegrams. She also informed him of William Wickham's visit to the Moffitt Farm. Wickham claimed that Johnny hadn't been truthful about certain affairs pertaining to the McClintock property. Several of the wells, including the Lone Star had run dry and Hamilton McClintock was in the process of selling the 'lower seven' to an oil prospector for a healthy sum. The angry businessman also advised Ellie that he had spoken to a judge in Franklin and was in the process of having the contract for the purchase of the farm annulled.

Confused and disturbed, Johnny angrily questioned the postmaster in regard to the missing telegrams. "Mister Steele, them letters been sent to your room at the Continental, just like you requested. Your partner, Mister Slickum, been acceptin' them. I personally delivered one to him just two or three days ago," the elderly man declared with a concerned look in his tired eyes.

Furious, Johnny rode back to his hotel room and tore the place apart looking for the telegram. Unsuccessful, he dashed down the hall to Slocum's room. He pushed the door open and found Slocum sound asleep. Johnny desperately searched the pockets of the snoring man's pants and suit jacket. He fumbled through the oak dresser and matching vanity drawers. The ruckus from the slamming dresser drawers was beginning to wake Slocum.

Steele got down on the floor and peered under the bed. He found what he was looking for. Several crumpled telegrams, one nearly three weeks old, were barely visible in the darkness. Johnny unraveled some of the little pieces of paper and read the messages in the light from a window. Ellie had been begging him to return home. She also told him that she loved and missed him and that her heart was breaking. Ellie was tired of oil and money and just wanted to be a family again.

Seth Slocum sat up in bed, rubbing the sleep from his eyes. He instantly recognized the hostility on Johnny's face. The furious young man tossed the crumpled telegrams onto the bed at Slocum's feet. Rage now clouded Steele's expression, and fear widened Seth Slocum's bloodshot eyes. "I can explain," he asserted defensively. "I'll bet you can't!" Steele shouted as he lunged and grabbed hold of Slocum's left ankle. With lightning speed, he yanked the smaller man from the bed, and Slocum's backside slammed onto the hardwood floor. Slocum gasped for air as the impact knocked the breath from his lungs. Johnny clutched him by the neck and lifted his slouching frame from the floor. He pulled Slocum's terrified face close to his. "Consider our partnership over!" He shouted as he struck the man squarely in the face with his clenched fist. Johnny felt the cartilage from the bridge of Slocum's nose give way under his knuckles. Slocum fell back several feet, landing on the bed and clutching his bleeding appendage. "You're fired!" Steele grimaced as he stormed out of the room.

CHAPTER 28

Johnny Returns to the Oil Region

An unseasonably warm spell for early February had arrived, and with it came John Washington Steele. Ellie and her parents welcomed him back with open arms. A few days after his return to the oil region, Johnny visited my new wife and me at our Franklin home. As gifts, he presented me with a finely-crafted gold watch, and he delighted my spouse with a beautiful diamond pendant. He expressed is sadness about missing our happy union.

Upon leaving my residence, Steele rode to the Venango County Court-house, where he'd been summoned by Judge William A. Galbraith. Also present were oneW. Wickham and Billy Blackstone. Wickham claimed that John W. Steele had misled him about the productivity of the McClintock Farm. He also claimed that the farm was in terrible disorder, and that Steele had received thirty-five thousand dollars as a loan until the deed for the farm was cleared. The shady businessman wanted his thirty-five grand back and another ten thousand in expenses for legal representation. He wanted the con-tract nullified, and an additional five-thousand dollars for travel and hotel accommodations.

Now Johnny had never promised Wickham anything other than the sale of the farm. However, the old conniver convinced the Judge that he was promised an oil farm with a dozen productive oil wells, and the entire plot as registered in the deed. He claimed that he had no knowledge of the "Lower Seven" until Steele agreed to sell the farm. Then it was John W. Steele's duty to secure the lower portion of the farm from Hamilton McClintock before the date of the final sale.

Wickham testified that upon his return from Philadelphia with the signed agreement, he found the farm in total disrepair. Johnny's former agent and farm caretaker claimed that during his service on the farm, several wells had dried up, and he hadn't been paid in nearly three months. Blackstone stated that he had received his last paycheck in early November, and by early February, had to seek employment elsewhere. He contended that his family was struggling to survive and that he had to work as a teamster to make ends meet. Billy Blackstone informed the Judge that Mr. Steele agreed to pay him one-thousand dollars a month to manage the property.

Though Johnny was steaming at Wickham's misleading testimony, he couldn't blame Blackstone for his bitter revelation. While in Philadelphia, Seth Slocum was supposed to be handling Steele's financial responsibilities, and was receiving a handsome salary to do so. As Johnny's assistant, Slocum was in charge of the payroll. Yet Slocum was better at spending Johnny's money than managing it. The Judge quickly ruled in Blackstone's favor. Steele expressed his regret in the way Blackstone had been treated, and when the Judge declared three thousand in restitution, Johnny offered four thousand dollars. Billy shook Johnny's hand in appreciation and left the courthouse a happy man.

The Judge then convened to his quarters for an hour before returning for the decision in Wickham's claim. In Wickham's favor, he ordered that Steele return the thirty-five thousand dollars for the original agreement. He then ordered Johnny to pay another ten-thousand in compensation for legal representation. Galbraith also charged Johnny with obstruction, and ordered him to pay another ten-thousand dollars for bond and legal fees.

The Judge then scolded Johnny for his unfair business practices and gave him one month to pay off his obligations. Steele barely had enough money in his reserves to pay the judgments. The McClintock Farm had two remaining leases that were still somewhat productive and would provide a source of income.

However, two weeks later Johnny was back in court. Henry Carnegie, proprietor of the Continental Hotel in Philadelphia, entered a judgment for nineteen-thousand dollars. E. Caldwell Jewelers and Lewis Ladomus Diamonds claimed Steele owed them eleven-thousand dollars for merchandise. Oakford Tailors submitted an unpaid bill for fifteen-hundred dollars.

The firm of Field and Collender wanted another fifteen-hundred dollars for the purchase of a billiard room which Steele's gambler friend, George Brotherton, had agreed to purchase. The Judge awarded settlements in all claims against Steele.

Disgusted and discouraged, Johnny left the courthouse and sought legal help from Taylor, Mackey and Company. Attorney James Mackey suggested that Johnny sell the McClintock Farm to pay off the judgments. Mackey felt that the farm still had substantial value, considering that there were two productive wells and that the railroad was looking to purchase property in the region.

Too upset to return home to the Moffitt Farm, Johnny climbed onto his favorite steed and journeyed back to the McClintock Farm. Three hours later, the sun was dipping beyond the horizon. Sleep came upon him with the help of a quart of whiskey stashed behind the pantry.

FORTUNE TURNS

CHAPTER 29

Falling Upon Hard Times

It was another fair morning when Johnny awoke from the bed in which he had slept as a boy. Just outside the bedroom window he could hear the raspy chatter of several black-capped chickadees as they darted about a barren elderberry bush searching for nourishment. The commotion of a train could be heard in the distance as several carloads of oil barrels were being transported to Titusville from Oil City along the newly erected Oil Creek railroad. The hustle and bustle of the regular oil trade was taking the day off as it usually did on the Sabbath.

Johnny lay awake in bed for nearly an hour while reflecting on the judgments brought against him the previous day. Distraught about possibly losing the farm through his own irresponsibility and trust of so-called friends, he flung himself out of bed and stumbled into the kitchen. There he set a pot of water onto the wood stove to boil for coffee.

Before the kettle started to whistle, Johnny thought he heard an approaching horseman. He dropped the pot of hot water onto the floor and dashed down into the cellar, where he removed a small, cherry-wood box from a shelf stacked with mason jars. He pressed a tiny brass button at the front of the finely crafted piece, and the lid sprung upward, revealing a short-barreled Colt .44-caliber revolver.

A bullet mold, a flask of powder, a canister of percussion caps, and a dozen bullets surrounded the pistol in the crimson, velvet-lined case. Steele removed the finely balanced revolver and examined it to make sure it was still loaded before he stuffed it into the belt near his hip. He then quietly proceeded to the front door of the farmhouse and he pressed his ear up against the rough wood surface. At the sound of stealthily approaching footsteps, Steele yanked the revolver from his waistband, held it at his hip and kicked open the door.

Bright sunlight exploded into the room. Steele's first reaction was to shield his eyes against the haze of light and dust particles. "Are you gonna shoot me?" a stern yet sweet voice demanded. In the doorway stood the shadowed figure of a woman. Johnny lowered the forearm that protected his eyes and saw his beautiful wife. Her golden hair glistened in the sunlight and her olive complexion radiated warmth. "When you didn't come home yesterday, I got worried."

The anguish from the previous day's proceedings were forgotten, for before him stood the most precious thing in his life. No amount of wealth could take the place of Ellie. She had stuck with him through thick and thin, and had never lost faith in him. Johnny bolted forward and embraced her in his arms. "God, I love you!" he said as he pulled her in close.

Johnny informed Ellie of the hearing and the further judgments brought against him. He wept at the prospect of selling his inheritance because of debts. Eleanor comforted him and suggested that he transfer the deed to her name. She rationalized that in doing so, the farm would be protected from seizure by the court and sold at auction. Ellie felt that the remaining leases on the property were still productive enough to liquidate the debts and support the family as long as Johnny and Ellie moved back to the McClintock Farm and managed it themselves.

Now Johnny knew that Ellie didn't want to stay in the oil region and work on a farm, but her devotion and loyalty were enough to keep him going. Her optimism, wit, and compassion made him feel that young Eleanor Moffitt-Steele was actually Sarah McClintock reincarnate.

Several leases located just two miles north of the McClintock Farm were producing a thousand barrels a day. Wildcat hollow became one of the most productive plots in the region. It was so productive that the price of oil per barrel fell dramatically over the course of several weeks. At one point, the price of a gallon of oil went from 75 cents to 22 cents in less than six weeks.

Though the price of crude oil was falling, the new technology was raising productivity. The railroads and newly constructed pipelines were lowering the cost of transportation. Steam engine pumps had been abandoned for more powerful gasoline engines, and some of the new wells were producing nearly four thousand barrels a day.

In 1865 Petroleum Center was still in its heyday, but several miles to the north, a much greater boomtown was rising in an enormous buckwheat field near Titusville. By fall of 1865 this metropolis would become one of the most famous oil towns in history. Pithole City was born.

CHAPTER 30

Pithole City

The following Spring brought both jubilation and anguish. On April 9th, Lee surrendered to Grant, thus ending the Great War and the South's secession. Less than a week later the President was assassinated while attending a play in Washington. The North greatly mourned the loss of their Commander-in-Chief. Never before or since has there been a more morally upright and courageous man than Abraham Lincoln. It was a difficult time for the newly resurrected nation.

The Steele family had also fallen upon difficult times. More judgments were brought against young Steele. His enormous spending sprees during the Philadelphia career were inevitably going to cost him the farm.

There was much excitement about some productive plots of land surrounding a newly constructed boomtown near Titusville. Johnny felt that if he could acquire some land and drill a couple of productive oil wells, the McClintock Farm would be spared.

One early June day, Johnny boarded a train and traveled to Titusville. At the depot, he caught the next stage out. The stagecoach followed a freshly cleared road that meandered through stony buckwheat fields and rocky glens darkened by massive hemlocks. The roar of the rushing Pithole Creek could be heard in the distance. The earthen, stump-riddled road was congested with other coaches, oil wagons, and pedestrians. Six miles later, the road branched off into three separate directions. Fifty-foot tall derricks came into view, as all the trees overlooking the valley had been reduced to stumps. The familiar mechanical pounding of pumping engines and the pungent odor of crude oil filled the air. Scores of oil men tended to their leases while others cleared land along the creek for the railroad. As the stagecoach crested the hill, the greatest boomtown in the Oil Region came into view. The metropolis known as 'Pithole City' and its fifteen-thousand residents made the other towns look like mining camps in comparison. Construction had begun just a few months earlier when a gusher of a well was drilled near the Holmden farm. Two more liquid gold mines were struck shortly thereafter, and soon after word got out, the oil prospectors moved in to buy up the land. The shantytown contained sixty hotels, a dozen mercantiles, several theatres, and two telegraph offices.

The saloon district contained several drinking establishments and nearly as many brothels. The City had its own fire department and newspaper, and housed the largest post office in the county.

The muddy streets were full of hustle and bustle as hordes of people arrived daily. Carpenters, stone masons, boiler makers, and refiners followed the oil trade here to seek employment. Businessmen and oil prospectors clad in fine suits came in from big cities like Pittsburgh, Buffalo, and New York. Lines of mud-splattered oil wagons driven by hardy teamsters labored through the upgrade on the far side of the valley on their way to the oil depots in Corry.

Long lines of hungry men waited for hot meals at the local eating establishments, while others eagerly awaited the whiskey wagons from Oil City. Dozens of uprooted souls gathered at the Post Office, hoping for letters from loved ones back at home.

The stage deposited Johnny and the other passengers at the depot on Holmden Street. The sloppy avenue was congested with pedestrian and wagon traffic. In the absence of decent sanitation, the streets reeked of rotting garbage and manure. Small clouds of black flies swarmed the passers-by, causing much irritation. Steele gawked at the Chase House, an eighty-thousand dollar enterprise that rivaled some of the finer hotels in Philadelphia and New York. The three-story building's catwalks were lined with nosey tenants basking in the warm midday sun. Just north of the Chase was a boot and shoe store, and the aroma of freshly tanned leather momentarily eclipsed the stench of the street.

Johnny trudged past a grocery and a tailor shop before he found the Land Leasing Office. To his discouragement, there was a long line of men standing along the boardwalk in front of the whitewashed box shanty, prospectors like himself hoping to lease a plot and strike it rich. The gossip among several bystanders centered around the cost of the endeavor. The newly formed Central Petroleum Company was charging several hundred dollars for leasing each half-acre plot and ten percent on each barrel of oil sold.

After a short while, a tall, pale fellow wearing a black stovepipe hat pushed his way out of the office. He announced to the crowd that he was not accepting any more bids, since all of the plots had been spoken for. The gaggle of humanity sighed and uttered a few expletives before scattering onto the street. As a disappointed John Steele stepped away from the crowd, someone hollered, "Coal Oil Johnny! Hey! It's Coal Oil Johnny!" Another person eyed Steele. "Yeah! I'd recognize him anywhere! That's John Steele! Oil prince and millionaire!" A whole crowd of spectators were gawking at him. "Why are you wearin' them rags?" a woman asked in reference to his dingy flannel shirt and mud-stained britches.

Johnny was fuming. Upon returning to the Oil Region he had shed the fancy suits, diamond-studded pendants, gold watches, and chains for more appropriate attire. A larger crowd started to gather around the young man. "So you're the legendary Coal Oil Johhny?" another fellow asked. "Don't look like no Oil Tycoon too me!" he added. Johnny wanted to ring his scrawny neck. Somewhere from near the back of the crowd one gent was telling another that he had seen Johnny in New York City and claimed that Steele purchased the exquisite Fifth Avenue Hotel. The loudmouthed fool also claimed that Johnny was one of the wealthiest men in the world and often supped with kings and queens.

Just as Johnny was about to deny his identity, the blunt figure of a man pushed his way through the gaggle. In a loud and stern voice he demanded that they break it up. "Git movin'! Let's go!" the sheriff ordered as the loiters dispersed. The brawny fellow then approached Steele. Perspiration glistened on the angry law officer's forehead while thick veins about his temples throbbed with adrenaline. "Any more crap like that and I'll have you transported to the County Jail!" The sheriff then raised his stubby index finger and thrust it forward at Steele's nose. "Don't be disturbin' no peace in this town, boy!" He then lowered his finger and stepped back. "Now git!" he shouted as Johnny turned and went about his way.

The commotion had drawn much attention. At the corner of Holmden and Prather Streets was the Erie and Buffalo Saloon. In front of the saloon stood George Croyle and Stonehouse Jack Thompson. Croyle had arrived in Pithole just a few days earlier. He had left Petroleum Center when word spread that a band of vigilantes was looking to lynch him. The outlaw was being accused of robbing and murdering John McFate. McFate was a highly respected citizen in the Oil Creek region who had just received a good sum of money for the sale of his farm. He was slain on the road back from Oil City. There was no doubt in most people's minds that Croyle was the guilty party. It was also believed that Croyle and his new-found accomplice, Stonehouse Jack, had robbed John Benninghoff of a half-million dollars.

Benninghoff's armed guard had been overpowered and the safe stolen. The heavy iron box was never recovered, but the guard's battered and bloodied body was found the following day in an abandoned pumphouse in Wildcat Hollow. It didn't take a genius to figure out that it would take men of enormous stature and physical power to pull off such a feat. Benninghoff notified the U.S. Marshal's Office and offered a mighty sum of cash for justice. Six well-armed and experienced lawmen would be arriving shortly.

Croyle was aware of this, but before fleeing the region, there was a personal vendetta he wanted to resolve.

CHAPTER 31

Outlasting Outlaws

After securing a room at the Tremont Hotel for the evening, Johnny figured he'd vent his frustration from making the long, fruitless journey by visiting a local tavern. Since returning from Philadelphia several months earlier, Steele had pretty much steered clear of liquor. Drinking water was scarce in Pithole, for most of the springs and streams in the area were contaminated with oil and sludge. A glass of water cost nearly twice as much as a pint of beer or a shot of whiskey. Therefore, Johnny was justified in having a couple of cold beers to quench both his thirst and frustration.

Leaving the hotel, Johnny followed the mud-splattered boardwalk down onto First Street and into the saloon district. He proceeded through a long, shaded alley and stepped into the Lacer Saloon. The Lacer was different from the other drinking establishments in the city. There were no tables or chairs for eating or gambling. The proprietor served only draught beer. Unlike the other saloons that offered whiskey and faro games, the little whitewashed shanty drew meager crowds.

Johnny proceeded to the bar where he was approached by a couple of disreputable girls. He gave them a cold shoulder and ordered a beer. The beer was warm, but he struck up an interesting conversation with the barkeep. A few minutes later a big, burly fellow limped into the saloon. An unsightly gent, a large scar ran from his forehead just above the temple down across his cheek, before disappearing into his scraggly gray beard. He wore a Union frock, and the leather sheath at his waist contained a massive Bowie knife. Johnny figured him for a war veteran.

In a deep, growling voice, the old sergeant demanded a beer. Clearly intimidated by the big man, the friendly but diminutive bartender worked urgently in pouring a beer from the tap to satisfy his unnerving patron. The husky man was so intimidating that even the saloon girls dare not approach him. Of course, that might also have had something to do with the stench and filth that surrounded his massive frame.

Three beers later, Johnny noticed that the sun was beginning to slip below the horizon. A shadow was cast upon the city, and most of the businesses about town were closing up for the evening. A couple of teamsters and a grimy lease operator straggled in to quench their thirst. Steele had struck up another conversation with the timid bartender. Ely Peete haled from nearby Corry, Pennsylvania. His family operated a large mercantile There. When word spread about Pithole and the wealth surrounding the oil trade, he jumped onto the bandwagon and rushed into town to purchase a lease. He got swindled and outbid by another fellow, and instead of returning to his family in shame, he invested his savings in the Lacer. Since drinking water was scarce, he figured that beer was a good investment. Though he refused to serve whiskey and other evil spirits, he had six different kinds of beer on tap. He had imported beer that was brewed as far away as St. Louis, Missouri. Peete wasn't going to make a fortune, but he was making a profit and had gained a gratifying independence from his high-achieving parents and siblings.

Johnny knew what it was like to be swindled. He was struggling to hold onto the McClintock farm, and he could relate well with the undaunted little bartender. Peete had named the saloon after his intended bride: Lacey Bissell. Lacey's father was kin to oil tycoon and millionaire George Bissell. He had acquired a speech impediment after suffering a head injury during a boiler explosion. Therefore he addressed his daughter as Lacer hence the name.

Peete was familiar with most of the local gossip and goings-on in the boomtown. He quietly identified the big, ugly man as Stonehouse Jack Thompson. Thompson was a ruthless thug who was believed to have beaten and robbed at least three people since his recent arrival in Pithole City. He had never fought in the Great War, and was rumored to have killed a much-decorated Union veteran just for his uniform. Jack was now portraying himself as a veteran to deceive the local law and potential victims.

The barkeeper surprised Steele by informing him that Jack was keeping a low profile since Ben Hogan and French Kate had arrived. Hogan and his fiery, hot mistress had closed shop in Petroleum Center and moved to the greener pastures and wealthier clientele of the great new city. They were operating a large saloon and brothel on the north side of the district.

A few nights earlier, a drunken Stonehouse Jack Thompson had stumbled into Hogan's Brothel and badly beat up one of the girls when she refused his advances. Hogan confronted Thompson and beat him down in the middle of the street. Hogan gave Jack a week to leave town before he'd kill him with his bare hands. In return, Stonehouse Jack vowed revenge and intended to kill Hogan before his departure from Pithole City.

"Git me another beer, boy!" Thompson shouted, bringing an end to the engaging conversation. He then focused on young Steele with an unpleasant grimace. Peete handed Jack another mug of beer. The big man engulfed the beverage in seconds. He then smashed the thick glass mug on the hardwood bar before reluctantly tossing a small wad of cash down to cover his tab. He eyeballed the bartender and snarled at Johnny before staggering out the door. "That is one vile S.O.B.!" the bartender remarked, delighted that Jack and his stench were gone for the evening. As the revolting big man's darkened shape faded into the night, another gent stumbled into the saloon. Johnny recognized the face, but couldn't quite recall the man behind it. The tall, lanky fellow ordered a beer. When his raspy, obnoxious voice echoed through the room, Johnny remembered. It was the loudmouthed pedestrian who had created the commotion in the street earlier in the day, the same big mouth that had nearly gotten Steele arrested.

Johnny really didn't care to be made a spectacle of again, so he paid his tab, bade farewell to Peete, and discreetly stepped out the door. When he stepped onto the street he noticed a looming, orange glow toward the far end of town. He could see the distant reflections of pulsating light against the backdrop of buildings and trees, and fiery embers cascading high into the blackened sky. Moments later a huge water wagon pulled by a team of eight horses dashed up the street. Johnny could barely make out the letters forming Pithole Fire Brigade on the side of the massive barrel.

A pedestrian alerted the others that another well had caught fire and had spread to a stable on the north end of town. Fires were an everyday occurrence in a city built around crude oil. The street was now crowded with spectators trying to catch a glimpse of the giant bonfire.

More water wagons rumbled by as anxious firemen hollered for pedestrians to get out of the street. Their language was as foul as any broken-down teamster but who could blame these men of great courage. Theirs was an occupation more dangerous than any, other than maybe a peace officer's.

Abandoning the busy street, Johnny opted for the alley behind the saloon to get back to the Tremont. It was pitch-black in the long corridor, so Johnny struck a match; but as he raised the tiny torch, he was startled by a sudden presence from behind. When he reached for the pistol buried under the sash at his hip, he was grabbed with tremendous force and shoved several feet forward. Someone pushed him again and again until he was far from the street. As Johnny staggered to his feet, a huge man picked him up and slammed him to the ground.

Another match flickered and when a lantern was lit, a disturbing image took shape; the illuminated face of the Goliath that Johnny had smitten in Petroleum Center two years prior. The bible's David disposed of his Goliath properly because he never came back, but Johnny wasn't as fortunate.

In the dim light of the lantern was the enraged face of George Croyle. The monster of a man twirled a hickory axe handle in his right hand. Still aware of a presence behind him, Johnny cautiously stood to his feet. "Remember me, boy?" Croyle angrily shouted. "You made me look a fool when you sucker-punched me in my head! Now you're gunna pay!" The hostility on Croyle's face alone was enough to kill a person. The big man raised the axe handle and lunged forward. With lightning speed, Steele yanked the Colt's revolver from under the red sash at his hip, thumb cocked the hammer, and fired.

The axe handle flew high into the air and the big man toppled forward. His 260 lb. frame plummeted onto Johnny as the two fell to a heap on the ground. Croyle was clutching his right foot in agony as a terrible burning sensation shot up through his massive leg. The .44 caliber ball had torn through the leather boot and penetrated the top of the foot just below the ankle. The lead projectile splintered a couple of bones and severed some nerves before lodging in the foot near the heel. Croyle screamed in pain as Johnny pushed him aside.

As Johnny reached for the revolver that was now on the ground at his side, another huge shadow materialized. "Leave it, boy!" Stonehouse Jack ordered, clutching a large Bowie knife above Johnny's head. Jack raised the long knife and was about to carve Johnny up when another large man appeared out of the darkness. A mighty fist shot through the shadows, striking Jack squarely in the temple. The impact produced an impressive thud and the knife-toting ruffian collapsed to the ground.

Still clutching his wounded foot, Croyle staggered to his feet and retreated into the blackness of the alley ahead. Ben Hogan stepped out of the shadows and helped Steele to his feet. Johnny retrieved the revolver and stuffed it back under the dusty and torn sash. Hogan examined the boy's face and recognized him from Petroleum Center.

Hogan smirked. "Damn, boy! You need to quit mixin' it up with these no-good outlaws. If you keep whoopin' my challengers, it's gonna come down to me and you! Now I ain't never lost a fight, and I aim too keep it that way!" the champion chuckled. Before Steele could thank the prizefighter-businessman, the Sheriff stepped into the alley. He nodded at Hogan and examined the heap known as Stonehouse Jack. He then turned to Johnny. "You again, boy!" he angrily remarked.

"It's alright, Bob. This thug tried to rob the lad," Hogan informed the antsy lawman. "Well, why didn't you say so?" the clueless Sheriff asked as he returned his revolver to the holster. Somewhat intimidated by Hogan's presence, the Sheriff turned and faded back into the darkness.

Johnny left town early the next morning. Two days later the Pithole Daily Record printed a story about Coal Oil Johnny: 'The Wealthiest Oil Tycoon in the Nation, Spotted in Drab Clothing along the City's Streets'. The same edition posted another story about an unidentified, scrawny young fellow who thwarted a robbery by single-handedly whipping two notorious Pithole City outlaws.

The Bandits George Croyle and Jack Thompson were never seen again in the oil region. Some speculated that they left to evade the U.S. Marshals. Others claim that they fled in fear. In fear of a pistol-toting angel sent by God to clean up the streets of a lawless town.

CHAPTER 32

The Legend Begins

The McClintock Farm was eventually sold at a reasonable price and Johnny was freed from debt. He was hired on by the Oil City and Titusville Railroad, where he worked for a few years before relocating his family to the Midwest. His family settled in Lincoln, Nebraska, where he was employed by both the railroad and a local merchant who operated a large grocery store. I hadn't heard from him in nearly three decades. Just after the turn of the century, in 1901, he arrived in Franklin. He was now a man of fifty-eight years. The folds of skin that hung under his eyes and the clammy, sunken cheeks, revealed a tired and nearly defeated soul. John's health was beginning to fail him, though he had given up tobacco and liquor several years earlier.

He had returned to the region to write a book, a volume that would both confirm and deny much of what the newspapers and tabloids had written about him over the years. More than three decades after Steele had squandered his fortune, people were still fabricating stories about his life. Some parents even tried to scare their children into living good, productive lives by repeating the story of Coal Oil Johnny and reminding them of the catastrophic results that come from living in such a foolhardy manner.

One morning during his short visit, John and I boarded the train in Franklin and enjoyed a ride into Rouseville. There we stopped off at the depot located just above the old Rynd Farm. By now, John D. Rockefeller and his Standard Oil Company owned the oil trade. The bustling town of Rouseville had been built on several farms, including my father's, after Rockefeller agreed to pay a fair price for the property.

Johnny and I spent some time in town attempting to locate old friends. Unfortunately, most of our comrades had departed after Rockefeller and his enormous wealth moved in and bought them out. We eventually ambled down to the creek, where the railroad had recently constructed a bridge right over one of my favorite boyhood fishing holes.

We cautiously stepped along the thick wooden ties until we neared the center of the iron-clad bridge. Nearly three stories above the surface of the crooked waterway, John peered out over the past. Just above us was the property that had once been the McClintock Farm. Standard Oil had purchased most of the land, other than the old Farmhouse, which was being used by the lease operator and tenant, John Waitz. My father had sold the Buchanan farm several years earlier, and it was now a part of the burrough of Rouseville. In fact, two hotels and a saloon were built on the stony plot that my father had cleared more than forty years earlier for planting crops.

Tears welled in John's eyes and rolled down across his waxy cheeks as he reminisced about his family. He recalled the first time Culbertson McClintock took him fishing, and how proud he was of the young boy when he caught a trout. How his beloved sister Permelia tiptoed her way along the rocky embankment gathering blackberries or searching for gems with her constant companion, Sarah Rynd. He even recalled the first time he fell and bruised his knee, and how Sarah McClintock took him into her arms and comforted him. Her voice was as soothing as a cool breeze on a warm day, and she loved to laugh, especially at Johnny's pranks.

"I failed them, Andrew. My recklessness all those years ago cost me the farm and their memories." I could feel his pain. "I'm the laughingstock of the entire oil region. Hell, there's a store in Oil City that sells Coal Oil Johnny soap," he added while wiping his face with a handkerchief. I told him that no one could have endured all his trials at such a tender age. Most of his family members had died before he was 21, so how could he avoid a tendency to live on the edge? I reminded him of the courage he exhibited on numerous occasions when we were kids. He was never a man of large stature but John Washington Steele's cunning and fearlessness had helped him overcome overwhelming odds.

With that reassurance the color slowly returned to his face. He thanked me for the sentiments and said good-bye to the spirits of his family. "You know, Drew. You don't see the rattlesnakes anymore. Not like when we were youngsters," Johnny noted while gazing over the meandering creek. "You sure don't, Johnny." We both laughed.

John returned to the Midwest, where he overcame his illness and lived another two decades. When he died in 1921, John Washington Steele was seventy-eight.

Over the years the story of Coal Oil Johnny and his spendthrift ways has been told and retold. Old newspaper clippings show up here and there, reminders of the fabricated tales people used to tell. However, in the hearts of those who truly knew and admired him, Johnny deserved his status as a legend …

REFERENCES

1. Steele, John W.—'Coal Oil Johnny-His Book' Franklin, PA: Mongs 1902

2. Szalewicz, Steve S.—'Oil Moon Over Pithole' 1958

3. Flaherty, Kathy and Thomas—'Oil and Gas in PA'

Special thanks to the Drake Well Museum located in Titusville, Pennsylvania for your Wonderful models and wealth of information regarding the oil boom.

978-0-595-45232-3
0-595-45232-9

Printed in the United States
82637LV00004B/478-495/A